D1363296

This book should Lancashire County Library of the shown

SCS

8 SEP 2008

25 SEP 2008

10 OCT 2008

2 0 NOV 2008

0 5 JAN 2009

- 2 MAR 2009

1 4 APR 2009

2009

- 9 SEP 2009

- 8 MAY 2010

2 1 MAR 2011

CSH 06/11

- 1 AUG 2012

2 7 MAR 2013

1 8 APR 2016

2 1 MAY 2016

3 0 DEC 2016

1 4 JUL 2017

JUL 2018

Lancashire County Library
Bowran Street
Preston PR1 2UX

www.lancashire.gov.uk/libraries

Lancashire County Library

30118109912208   LL1(A)

SPECIAL MESSAGE TO READERS

This book is published under the auspices of

THE ULVERSCROFT FOUNDATION

(registered charity No. 264873 UK)

Established in 1972 to provide funds for research, diagnosis and treatment of eye diseases. Examples of contributions made are: —

A Children's Assessment Unit at Moorfield's Hospital, London.

•

Twin operating theatres at the Western Ophthalmic Hospital, London.

•

A Chair of Ophthalmology at the Royal Australian College of Ophthalmologists.

•

The Ulverscroft Children's Eye Unit at the Great Ormond Street Hospital For Sick Children, London.

You can help further the work of the Foundation by making a donation or leaving a legacy. Every contribution, no matter how small, is received with gratitude. Please write for details to:

THE ULVERSCROFT FOUNDATION,
The Green, Bradgate Road, Anstey,
Leicester LE7 7FU, England.
Telephone: (0116) 236 4325

In Australia write to:
THE ULVERSCROFT FOUNDATION,
c/o The Royal Australian and New Zealand
College of Ophthalmologists,
94-98 Chalmers Street, Surry Hills,
N.S.W. 2010, Australia

THE FROZEN LIMIT

Defying the edict of the Medical Council, Dr. Robert Cranston, helped by Dr. Campbell, carries out an unauthorised medical experiment with a 'deep freeze' system of suspended animation. The volunteer is Claire Baxter, an attractive film stunt-girl. But when Claire undergoes deep freeze unconsciousness, the two doctors discover that they cannot restore the girl. She is barely alive. Despite every endeavour to revive the girl, nothing happens, and Cranston and Campbell find themselves charged with murder . . .

JOHN RUSSELL FEARN

THE FROZEN LIMIT

Complete and Unabridged

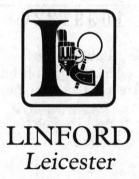

LINFORD
Leicester

First published in Great Britain

First Linford Edition
published 2008

Copyright © 1954 by John Russell Fearn
Copyright © 2003 by Philip Harbottle
All rights reserved

British Library CIP Data

Fearn, John Russell, *1908 – 1960*
    The frozen limit.—Large print ed.—
Linford mystery library
    1. Medicine, Experimental—Fiction
    2. Medical personnel—Malpractice—Fiction
    3. Medical ethics—Fiction 4. Suspense fiction
    5. Large type books
    I. Title
    823.9′12 [F]

    ISBN 978–1–84782–301–4

1099122O8 CSH 06/11

Published by
F. A. Thorpe (Publishing)
Anstey, Leicestershire

Set by Words & Graphics Ltd.
Anstey, Leicestershire
Printed and bound in Great Britain by
T. J. International Ltd., Padstow, Cornwall

This book is printed on acid-free paper

1

Forbidden Experiment

Eva Cranston knew the moment her husband entered the lounge that his mission had failed. He had left the house that morning in the highest spirits — a young doctor with, as yet, an anything but flourishing practice — determined to at last place before the Medical Council the greatest discovery since Lister had discovered antiseptic.

Nothing less than bloodless surgery, produced by suspended animation and absolute cessation of molecular movement — or at least, almost complete cessation. Not yet had Dr. Robert Cranston solved the problem of absolute material rest.

'Nothing doing?' Eva asked, as her husband mooched into the lounge, hands thrust deep into his trousers pockets.

'Not a sausage! They didn't laugh

outright, bless 'em, but they did hover on the verge of suggesting that I ought to be either certified or rested from practice. Rested! Great heavens, I've hardly enough patients to keep me occupied!'

Dr. Robert Cranston sat down and Eva looked at him and sighed. She had never been fool enough to think that becoming the wife of a struggling doctor would be a bed of roses, but she had thought there would be something worthwhile. Now she was commencing to doubt it. Her husband's practice was woefully small; he himself was not a particularly brilliant medical man . . . But he was a scientist with distinct medical leanings, and so far these two co-related states had somehow not teamed up very satisfactorily.

'No hope of them giving you a second chance?'

Cranston laughed shortly. 'My dear girl, once the M.C. has given its decision it never changes it. The whole thing's over and done with — far as they are concerned, anyway.'

'Which means you'll have to give up experimenting?'

Eva rose to her feet and came across to where her husband had dropped himself on the settee. She was as petite as he was big, and if it came to that as pretty as he was ugly. But Bob Cranston's ugliness was of the attractive kind. He had an all-over-the-place kind of face with a big, generous mouth. The contrast between the two — he dark and Eva fair — was about as absolute as it could be.

'No,' Bob Cranston said slowly as Eva sat beside him, 'I shall not give up experimenting. What would have happened if Lister had given up? Or Pasteur?'

'Yes, dear, but is your discovery so important after all? Most of the great things in surgery have already been discovered — such as anaesthetics and things. Why not give up this dabbling and confine yourself to bread and butter? After all we're not exactly rolling in wealth, are we?'

Bob grinned and clapped an arm about Eva's slender shoulders.

'Eva, my sweet, you're a grand girl, but you haven't a scientific bone in your body! Not for a moment do you realize the importance of slowing down the molecular vibration — '

'No, I'm afraid I don't.' Eva looked troubled. 'I keep thinking of the bank account and struggling to devise ways to make it bigger — only I just can't think of anything. You're the one who could make the money, only you don't.'

'I can't make people ill, sweetheart; nor can I make them come to me when they are.'

'Your heart isn't really in medicine, Bob, is it?'

He looked gloomy. ' 'Fraid not. I wouldn't have had anything to do with it at all but for dad insisting. Scientific research is my real line, and this molecular business really is something! It can put a patient under for as long as need be — years if required — and restoration is, or would be, simple. Thanks to the M.C, I'm not allowed to use anybody on whom to practice, and if I ignore that decision and try to go ahead I'll no longer be able to practice. Vicious circle — '

Eva glanced up as the front door bell

buzzed. Bob looked vaguely astonished and got to his feet.

'Wonder if by some miracle it's a patient?'

'Hardly! What's the surgery for? That was the front door.'

In another moment the rather faded-looking general help peered in the lounge, her bovine eyes traveling to Cranston.

'Who is it, Ella?'

'A Dr. Campbell, sir. Says it's very important and can you see him now?'

'Not as a patient I suppose?'

Ella shook her head. 'Didn't say so. Doesn't look like one, either. Big, well-setup man he is, and — '

'All right Ella thanks. Ask him to step into the surgery, will you? I'll be with him in a moment.'

'Yes, doctor.'

'I've not the vaguest idea what he can want,' Bob said as the door closed and Eva looked at him inquiringly. 'Unless by some extraordinary fluke the M.C. has reversed its decision and sent this blighter to tell me so.'

Eva did not look particularly hopeful.

'Easiest way to find out would be to see what he wants.'

'I know — but I don't believe in dashing to these fellow doctors. Creates a bad impression.'

For the life of her Eva could not see the point, but she did not stress the matter. She settled down more comfortably on the settee, then straightening his jacket Bob left the room, whisked on his white surgical overall from the hall wardrobe and finally entered the surgery with all the briskness of a famous surgeon about to perform a major operation.

The man waiting in the solitary hide armchair did not look impressed by this grand entrance. He was young, bony-kneed, with twinkling blue eyes and tumbled blond hair.

'Ah! Dr. Campbell!' Bob Cranston came forward as though he had made an epic discovery — and Campbell got to his feet. He was long and gangling, even taller than Bob, who topped the measure at six foot one.

'That's right — Boris Campbell. Remotely a Scot, born in London.' The handshake was powerful. 'Can you spare a moment to discuss?'

'Spare a moment? Well, I — er — ' Bob Cranston made noises in his throat and appeared to reflect. There was all the time in the world, of course, but it might not present a good impression if he were to say so.

'I can come back later,' Campbell volunteered anxiously.

'Great heavens no, old man. Since you've taken the trouble to come and see me we might as well finish it. My patients can wait. What's the trouble?'

'I'd hardly call it trouble, Dr. Cranston. I'm here because of that ridiculous farce at the Medical Council. I was in the audience even though I had no ruling vote.'

'Oh, I see.' Bob looked dubious; then he motioned to the armchair again and drew up a stool for himself.

'Those fossils on the M.C. Board want strangling,' Campbell announced refreshingly. 'You present the greatest idea of the century and ask for a volunteer to be permitted, and all you get is part ridicule and an absolute ban.'

'Uh-huh,' Bob agreed, sighing. 'So?'

'So this: I'm a medical man too, with about enough knowledge of science to grasp what you're driving at. Because of that, if you're prepared to take a risk, I think I can help you.'

'Risk?'

'Well, the Council did warn you that if you tried anything without permission you'd be liable to lose your practice.'

Bob grinned. 'You've no idea how funny that is, Dr. Campbell.'

'Oh, call me Boris. I'm sure we're good friends already. And how do you mean — funny?'

'It's funny because my practice is nearly non-existent on account of my scientific experiments. I spend so much time on scientific medical investigation I've no time to attend to those who are ill. The wife takes a very dim view of my activities.'

'Since your practice is small,' Campbell said, thinking, 'that makes it you have little to lose even if we fail — which we shan't — ' Then as Bob waited in puzzled silence Campbell hurried on: 'I've made several medical experiments in my time, chiefly on a small scale, and have been lucky enough to have had the Council's blessing each time. For those experiments I have hired the services of Jimmy Baxter, the human guinea pig. He is an amateur strong man, chief blood donor to the local hospital, and so bursting with good health he's a doctor's despair. But his iron constitution makes him useful for experiments.'

'Mmm,' Bob Cranston murmured none too cheerfully.

'He only charges five hundred pounds a time, and for that you can do anything you like with him — within reason, of course. I have him sign a letter of exoneration before I start, in case something does go wrong and he gets killed. The long and short of it is, Cranston — or should it be Bob? — that Jimmy Baxter will be willing to be put into suspended animation for five hundred pounds.'

'You really think so?' Bob Cranston was definitely interested at last.

9

'I'll ring him up before I leave here and find out — always granting you're willing.' Boris Campbell's blue eyes were twinkling brightly. 'You see, it's this way. Once you have put Jimmy into suspended animation and shown that bloodless surgery is practicable the M.C. won't dare take any action against you for flouting their decision. The possibility is that they'll publish an apology for being so short-sighted and the world will be compelled to acknowledge that Cranston's system of bloodless surgery is the greatest advancement of modern medicine. If anything goes wrong — '

'Nothing will. Nothing can.'

'Good! If it does, though, the exonera-tion letter will clear you of manslaughter even though you'll inevitably lose your practice.'

Bob got to his feet and stood meditating for a moment or two. Then he looked back at the genial Campbell. In the brief time he had known this young and lanky medico he had come to like him immensely. He appeared to ring true in every respect — but most of all he was providing the one thing Bob most needed at the moment — encouragement.

'I can't think of any reason why I shouldn't take the risk,' Bob said finally. 'Are you sure Jimmy What's-his-name will do it? It's absolutely new, you know — suspension of molecular activity.'

'No need to worry about that. Jimmy will do anything I ask him, and we've known each other since being at school. Incidentally, he has a smashing sister — Claire. Strictly off the cuff, I keep in with Jimmy because I more than like his sister.'

'Very original,' Bob grinned.

'She's a stunt girl,' Campbell added rather vaguely. 'Blonde, absolutely forth-right, entirely without fear, and pretty as hell.'

'Mmm. Stunt girl? Meaning what?'

'Oh, that?' Campbell smiled. 'She's a stand-in for stars — female of course — who have to dive from cliffs, fall in raging fires, hang from bridges by their teeth, and so on. I tell you straight, Bob, Claire and her brother are the two most fearless people I've ever known. They live

together in a little flat in London here and
— But never mind all that. It's Jimmy
we're interested in. Let me see if I have
my facts right concerning this system of
yours, and if I have I'll give him a ring
and get his reaction.'

'Fair enough.' Bob sat down again on
the stool.

'As I see it, you propose by electrical
means to slow down the movement of
molecules, working on the principle that
the less molecular activity there is the
lower the temperature drops. Just as when
there is no molecular activity at all — as
in outer space — the thermometer
registers minus two-seventy-three Centi-
grade, or absolute zero?'

'That's it in a nutshell.' Bob looked
pleased. 'Thanks for having understood
my exposition so clearly at the M.C.
meeting.'

'What kind of electrical energy do you
propose to use? I'm not quite clear on
that.'

'Nothing original about the electrical
energy: it's the same in any language
— but it is known amongst electrical

experts that if you produce a dampening circuit, as it is called, you can retard the molecular speeds in any known substance. In a word, it puts a brake on them. In a sense, even frost is a dampening electrical circuit of sorts in that it slows up the molecular action of many objects, and most certainly brings water to a standstill and causes it to change to ice. In the case of a human being, or for that matter any living creature, the rate of molecular vibration is well known. All I had to do was work out by mathematics the exact amount of electrical retardation required to slow up the molecular speed and so produce a form of frozen life, within a fraction of death. Ticklish, but it can most certainly be done.'

Campbell nodded and got to his feet. 'That's good enough for me! Mind if I use your phone over there?'

'Mind! You're doing all this on my account, anyway! Incidentally, Boris, what's your stake in this?'

Campbell turned, his face seriously thoughtful. 'Matter of fact I have no stake

13

at all, as such. It's just that I'm interested in seeing that you get a square deal — which you are certainly not getting from the Medical Council. They want to be made to sit up, and this should do it. Privately, though,' Campbell admitted, 'I have something of a stake in it. The subject will be Jimmy Baxter, and when he emerges safely from the great experiment he'll come in for as much fame and praise as you will — and myself too in a lesser way. That will inevitably rebound on Claire and — Well, you can guess the rest.'

'The crushing of the nut with the sledgehammer,' Bob said gravely. 'Yes, I gather the drift. Okay, let's see what Jimmy Baxter has to say.'

Campbell nodded and turned to the telephone. Bob sat waiting, listening in a half-detached fashion to the one-sided conversation; then at length Boris Campbell rang off and returned across the surgery.

'He'll do it!' He clapped his big hands together. 'All you have to do is to say when and where and he'll present himself. He asks for one thousand pounds, though, in view of the fact that it's an unusually risky assignment. Far more complicated than anything I have ever asked him to do.'

'He'll get his thousand. I'm confident enough.'

'Good! I told him that.' Campbell reflected. 'There is nothing then to stop us getting busy whenever you're inclined. Any idea when that will be?'

'Tomorrow night,' Bob answered. 'Around seven o'clock. I haven't enough surgery cases to worry about, so I can go right ahead. How about you?'

'I'm at your disposal: I can fix things at my end. Er — you're married, I believe?' Campbell questioned, and Bob looked surprised.

'Certainly. Does it signify?'

'Not at all, but forgive me being impolite in any way if I ask if your wife is entirely to be trusted?'

Bob's jaw tightened for a moment, then he relaxed. 'Oh, I see what you mean! Will she talk about the experiment?'

'That is what I fear. Wouldn't do, you

know: wouldn't do at all.'

'There's a simple way round that. I shan't tell her anything. She doesn't know what you have come for, and I see no need to enlighten her. She takes a decidedly murky view of my concentration on scientific research at the expense of my patients. No imagination, you know. Few girls have, bless 'em.'

Campbell gave his good-humored, boyish grin. 'Then it's all settled, then. I'll go round and see Jimmy personally and tell him to be here at seven o'clock tomorrow night. Better still, I'll pick him up and bring him: save him searching for the place. And not a word to a soul! Obviously you can rely on me.'

'Obviously,' Bob smiled, and shook hands. 'And thanks for coming to the rescue. I think, with a similar idea in mind and with the same conviction of success, that Pasteur or Lister would have done just as I am doing.'

With which Boris Campbell took his departure and Bob returned to offer vague and roundabout explanations to Eva.

'Very unusual,' she said finally, 'for a doctor to seek you out for medical advice. Couldn't he find anybody nearer?'

'Possibly — but he decided on me.' Bob smiled complacently. 'Evidently my air of authority at the Medical Council impressed him favourably.'

'Mmm — evidently.' Eva certainly looked as though she would have liked that statement clarified, but no such offer was forthcoming. Bob Cranston had said all he intended to say, and from then on he waited anxiously for the following evening.

The next day, after making the round of his few patients, many of whom had read of his rebuff at the Medical Council and were not particularly confident of him any more because of it, he returned home and spent the entire afternoon in the surgery, where there was also the necessary electrical apparatus for his suspended animation experiment. He knew he was safe here for Eva never trod on his professional territory. The only 'family' visitor here was Ella, and she had no imagination beyond cleaning the floor and dusting the heavier instruments.

Eva, though, did wonder what was preoccupying her husband to such an extent. An unconvincing reference to 'complicated prescriptions' did not at all satisfy her. She knew enough of her husband's list of patients to realize that none of them needed anything that could not be purchased from the local chemist. Unless maybe this mysterious Dr. Campbell — ! Ah, that might be it. Perhaps he wanted something complicated. So, to a certain extent, Eva was satisfied again. It was not — at this stage — that she distrusted her husband in the slightest degree: she loved him too much for that, but like most women she liked to know exactly what was transpiring in her own sphere.

At seven o'clock Bob was completely ready, having fobbed Eva off with the excuse that Dr. Campbell himself was not the one who required treatment, but the man whom he would bring with him this evening. Eva probed no further, and rather than spend a dreary evening by herself she set off for the theatre. Since it was also Ella's night off it seemed to Bob Cranston that everything in the garden was decidedly lovely.

At seven o'clock, however, he received a shock. The front doorbell rang and Dr. Boris Campbell was on the step, his car at the gate. But of the man of stupendous strength there was no sign.

'What's happened?' Bob demanded, admitting Campbell into the hall. 'Where's Jimmy Baxter?'

Campbell spread his hands. All the bright lights had gone from his usually twinkling blue eyes.

'Indefinite postponement, I'm afraid. The very devil that it had to happen — '

'But what has happened, man? Don't just stand there and talk to yourself! I've been banking on this — '

'I know, I know. So have I. When I went for Jimmy this evening his sister informed me that he's in hospital. Something busted inside him when he lifted a double-decker bus by its front bumpers yesterday. He'll not be available for at least two or three months.'

Bob said nothing. He looked woodenly

in front of him, feeling that this was the bitterest defeat of his life.

'Two or three months will be long enough for the Medical Council to forget it ever considered my plea. You realize that, Boris, don't you?'

'Man alive, I realize everything — only too well. I thought it only right that I could come over right away and tell you. I'm trying to cudgel my brains to think of somebody else who might fill the bill. Isn't easy though. It isn't everybody who's willing to be put into suspended animation.'

The observation was comic, but Campbell did not realize it. He and Bob looked at each other dully under the hall light.

'Come inside, anyway,' Bob invited finally.

'I am in, man!'

'I mean into the lounge. We may as well have a drink whilst we think out what comes next.'

Campbell nodded morosely and followed Bob into the lounge.

'The wife's at the theatre.' Bob tossed the information over his shoulder as he poured out drinks. 'Maid's out too — so we can be miserable together without interruption.'

'Umph,' Campbell agreed — and presently drank deeply. Then he said: 'You know, I feel personally responsible for this debacle. My promises caused you to build up your hopes, and now I've had to smash them all! I told Claire — Jimmy's sister, you know — to advise me if she could think of anybody to take Jimmy's place. Might be able to do something. In her line of work she meets all kinds of strange people.'

'She knew what Jimmy was going to do, then?'

'Naturally — and for whom. I can't be sorry enough, old man. I was quite looking forward to taking the starch out of those cocksure medical buzzards — '

A remote buzzing interrupted Campbell. He frowned and looked about him.

'Front door,' Bob explained, rising. 'If by some chance it is the wife come back, don't say too much. I've told her you are bringing me a patient — Jimmy Baxter — for special treatment.'

Bob was in the hall by the time he had finished his statement. He opened the front door, wondering who could be calling, then he stood staring blankly, and suddenly felt that it was good to be alive — Jimmy Baxter notwithstanding.

'Good evening,' the girl said in the sweetest voice, and her breath floated away on the stinging winter air.

'Good evening, madam.' Bob was suddenly formal. 'The surgery door is at the side. If you will — '

'I'm not here for that purpose. I'd like a private word with you — and Dr. Campbell if he's here.'

'Oh?' Bob looked at her again. She was pretty to the point of being devastating. Tip-tilted nose, merry grey eyes, pink cheeks — natural apparently — and curly wisps of golden hair peeping under her ridiculous apology of a hat.

'I'm Claire Baxter,' she explained, and Bob hardly heard what she said for he was concentrated upon her magnificent white teeth.

'And it's a cold night,' she added cheerfully.

'Yes — bitter.' Bob started. 'Oh, I'm so sorry! Miss Baxter! Of course! Jimmy Baxter's sister.'

'That's it. Is Dr. Campbell here? He said he was coming to break the bad news — '

'Sure he's here. Do come in, Miss Baxter. I'm all mixed up this evening.'

The girl smiled again, bewitchingly, and Bob had to admit as he closed the door that his thoughts could not have been further from Eva than at that moment. There was an aroma of elusive perfume in the air. Claire Baxter was everything a woman should be — graceful, extremely pretty, and — as Campbell himself had said — entirely forthright. She did not take advantage of her sex by shrinking into herself and only peeping out when it suited her.

'Claire, by all that's beautiful!' Boris Campbell rose to his gawky six-foot-four as the girl came into the lounge, her big winter overcoat well up around her ears. 'This is the one thing needed to make the evening complete! We're all alone here.'

'That a warning or an admission?'

Claire asked solemnly; then she turned as Bob followed her in. Immediately he motioned to the nearer armchair and the girl settled herself gracefully and unbuttoned her coat.

'Drink?' Bob invited — and Campbell hovered.

'No thanks. I daren't drink in my profession. One slip night finish me.'

'Which would be a terrible loss!' Campbell declared gallantly.

'To the film company I happened to be working for, yes,' Claire agreed. 'Otherwise I'm not sure — Anyhow to get down to cases. I'm here instead of my brother.'

Bob started and exchanged a quick glance with Campbell.

'Instead of — of Jimmy?' Campbell rubbed his top lip quickly. 'Well, now — Hmm! Let me think — '

'What about?' Claire asked frankly. 'You tried to hire Jimmy so he could be suspended, or something, and now he can't do it. All right. At the moment I'm resting between engagements and could do with some easy pickings. If I'm any use I'll do whatever it is you want for the same fee, and sign a letter of exoneration.'

'You know about that, then?' Bob asked, surprised.

'Naturally! Jimmy and I have no secrets from each other.'

'How ideal.' Bob smiled uneasily. 'Afraid it wouldn't work out though, Miss Baxter, much as we appreciate it. You see, you've hardly the kind of constitution which — '

'I'm not a superwoman, if that's what you mean, but I'm as strong in the general way as Jimmy is in his. I have to be in my work.'

Silence. Bob picked lint from his coat sleeves and looked broody. Campbell lowered his brows so much that he made his eyes disappear.

'After all,' he said presently, 'she is organic, old man. And she has molecules.'

'Pardon?' The deliciously pretty face was looking puzzled. 'Talking about me?'

'Professionally, Claire,' Campbell smiled. 'Just deciding if you might do.'

'Oh, I see — I think.'

Silence again. Then Bob jerked his head and Campbell followed him over into a corner of the lounge. Claire sat back and waited, crossing one shapely leg over the other.

'Viewed from strictly medical standards she'll certainly do,' Bob admitted. 'Excellent chance to see molecular reaction on the female. And naturally, bloodless surgery can be performed on women as much as men. Only thing is — '

'What?'

'The wife! This experiment will have to be performed in the surgery, and I'm convinced she won't believe it's strictly medical. If the girl looked like a battle-axe it would be okay, but as it is — I don't wonder you keep in with her brother!'

'You're dividing your allegiance between Cranston the man and Cranston the doctor and scientific experimenter,' Campbell murmured. 'This is all on the level, and Claire is the kind of girl to appreciate that.'

'Doubtless — but is Eva? That's my wife.'

'Mmm. Very well then, get rid of your wife!'

'What! What do you — '

'I don't mean murder her, man. Just

send her for a holiday. You're a doctor. Tell her she's going to pieces — anything you like. We can't afford to pass up a chance like this. Claire is the kind of girl who'll co-operate to the bitter end.'

Bob hesitated. The thing he most dearly wanted was the success of his experiment. That a ravishingly pretty girl had turned up as the subject instead of a male Hercules was not his fault after all. So —

'All right.' His voice was low but firm. 'We'll do it.'

Campbell nodded and they returned to where the girl was seated. She smiled up at them disarmingly.

'Finished muttering, boys?'

Bob looked a little taken aback, but the girl waved her hand gracefully.

'I don't stand on ceremony, you know. I'm used to dealing with camera crews, technicians, and all types. You two are boy friends to me even if you do hide behind your medical degrees. Well, what about it? Do I get suspended?'

'Certainly not.' Bob's voice was coldly formal — and very unconvincing.

'You have the system incorrectly, Miss Baxter — '

'Call me Claire. I hate stuffed-shirt talk.'

'The system,' Bob continued deliberately, 'is that of slowing down the bodily molecules and producing thereby a state of deep, frozen unconsciousness which is technically called suspended animation.'

'I knew something was suspended, and I thought it would be me. Well, why won't I do?'

'You will, Claire,' Campbell smiled. 'Bob here is just putting on a professional manner to convince you he is genuinely seeking a scientific result. The fact that you're a dashed pretty girl and entirely attractive has nothing to do with it.'

'I never thought it had. What queer ideas you boys get! Tell me more, Dr. Cranston — or is it Bob?'

Bob looked and felt warm. 'Once you are in a state of suspended animation I shall ask the Medical Council to study you,' he continued. 'When they are satisfied that my system is all that I claim for it I will revive you — and that will be that. You'll be hailed as the first subject of bloodless surgery, the pioneer who will bring new hope to millions as yet unborn.'

'Excellent,' Claire approved, clapping her hands. 'The next producer I see is going to hear about you. You've got dramatic possibilities. Right, so I'm to be put to sleep. Do you want me as I am, or stripped?'

Bob's eyes widened. 'Eh?'

'Well, I might as well know so I can — fix things. You needn't be shy: I'm used to being ordered to do the most astounding things.'

'I think,' Campbell said, musing and endeavoring to look detached, 'that your best policy would be to wear a swimsuit, Claire. I say that because testing of the reflexes — knees, elbow joints, and so on, will come into it — so the less covering, within the limit of decency, the better. Right?'

'I'm your man,' Claire agreed, smiling. 'When do we begin?'

'Well, I — er — ' Bob rubbed his ear and scowled.

'Tomorrow night at seven,' Campbell stated calmly. 'That will give you time to alter your domestic arrangements.'

'Uh-huh.' Bob looked as if he were about to leap into an icy river. 'You do understand what is expected of you, Miss — Claire, don't you?'

'Not entirely, but I trust you boys to the limit. You're going to make me unconscious, freeze me up, or something — and then whilst I'm not aware of it the medical boys will look me over with a microscope. That it?'

'Partly. All strictly medical, understand.'

'You needn't keep saying that. Just one thing: how do you produce this zero-sleep? Injection, cone on the face, or what?'

'Electrical,' Campbell hastened to explain. 'You will just pass into a deep sleep and will awaken a second later — or so it will seem to you.'

'Like the dentist's?'

'In a way.' Bob looked into her trusting gray eyes pensively. 'All facetiousness apart, Claire, I admire you immensely for taking this job on. You're a girl in a million. I'd try some other way, only I must have a human being, since it is human beings who will later reap the benefit.'

'I can already see the plaque in the world's biggest hospitals,' Claire smiled, getting to her feet. ' "In Honored Memory of Claire Baxter, to Whose Heroism we Owe Bloodless Surgery".'

'Could be,' Campbell admitted. 'Unless by then the name of Baxter is not in use.'

Claire gave him a quick glance and then looked back at Bob and held out her hand.

'Tomorrow night at seven, Bob. All complete in a swimsuit and my heart in my mouth — I don't think. Seeing me back home, Borry?'

'Be glad to — Oh, just a moment!' Campbell considered carefully; then, 'I'd better get in touch with Nurse Addison.'

'Oh?' Bob looked inquiringly. 'Who may she be?'

'She'll be chaperone on this job and make it ethical in case somebody tumbles on what we're doing and chooses to throw dirt. Nurse Addison is an ex-hospital matron and not bound by any of the M.C. rules. She's done a great deal for me at various times and can be relied upon to keep her mouth shut. Think I should get her, Bob?'

'S'pose so,' Bob sighed, thinking of his bank account. 'At least she'll make a trustworthy witness for later on, and probably Claire will feel more comfortable.'

Claire shrugged. 'Makes no difference. To me all this is a job of work, nurse or no nurse.'

'I'll get her anyway,' Campbell decided, and with that he ushered Claire before him to the door of the lounge.

2

Unexpected Developments

Bob was looking curiously benign when Eva returned from the theatre towards ten forty-five. So much so that over supper Eva could not help remarking upon it.

'Something happened?' she enquired, and Bob's generously ugly face broke into a serene smile.

'Oh, nothing vital. Just that I think Dr. Campbell and I are going to prove to that bone-headed Medical Council that my suspended animation system is workable enough.'

'Oh that!' Eva looked irritated. 'I thought you'd decided to give more attention to your practice?'

'I have, but after all I — ' Bob stopped, suddenly looking at Eva intently across the table. She stared back at him, vaguely startled.

'Any — anything the matter?'

'My dear, how ill you look!'

Eva started. 'Ill? Why, I never felt better! A little worried on account of your time-wasting perhaps, but — '

'Ah! And that worry is showing very clearly! Deathly pallor, rapid breathing, slight tremors of the hands and eyelids. Eva, you're in a shocking nervous condition.'

'Oh dear! Bob, do you honestly think so?'

He got up and came over to her, suddenly forcing back her lower eyelids with professional skill. Then he said:

'Mmm' — and reflected profoundly.

'Is it bad?' Eva insisted. 'Bob, you're a doctor. What's wrong with me? I feel fine, but of course I — '

'One often does feel fine before a complete collapse,' he said soberly. 'I think if we take this in time everything will be all right. Fool that I am! I've been so preoccupied with my work I've never noticed this thing creeping upon you — '

'What thing?'

'Never mind. Better you don't know. It

can be straightened out before you have a sudden and total collapse. Whatever it costs us you must go to the South of France for at least a month and do nothing but relax, sleep, and eat. That'll put you straight.'

Eva sighed. The idea of the South of France and escape from the rigours of the British winter was attractive enough: the cloud lay in not knowing what was wrong with her — and plainly Bob was maintaining professional secrecy about it.

'Yes, South of France!' he repeated firmly. 'I'll make the necessary arrangements this moment — and you my dear must leave tomorrow by the first available plane. Gosh, fool that I have been! Thank heaven I saw it in time.'

And to the South of France Eva went — at ten the following morning. Bob saw nothing wrong in what he had done. Eva would have every comfort and be safely out of the way. He regretted leaving a shadowy worry in her mind, but that could not be helped. Returning home he sent Ella packing — also for a month, with pay. Thuswise he cleared the decks for action.

Then it occurred to him that perhaps he had been a little too thorough. If the suspended animation experiment took a day or two to complete — first the descent into unconsciousness, then the demonstration to the M.C., and finally the awakening — there would be nobody to look after the domestic side, and it was pretty certain that Nurse Addison would not soil her hands with anything so menial.

'Aunt Bertha!' Bob told himself, snapping his fingers as the solution occurred to him. 'She's the one! Deaf as a post, willing as a horse — and about as intelligent — '

He fled immediately to the telephone. To his relief he was assured that Aunt Bertha would be there by five o'clock that afternoon, prepared to stay indefinitely. So that was that. For the rest of the day Bob had little to do but check his instruments again and wait patiently for the hours to pass by. He had to keep a hold on himself too, and remember he was a married man. Silly to keep thinking how attractive Claire Baxter was instead of concentrating on the essential details of his task.

By five o'clock however, he was as sedate as usual and took the car to the station to pick up Aunt Bertha. She was the same as she had looked at Christmas — stolid, broad, immovable, with an almost music-hall genius for misconstruing sentences aimed at her leaden ears.

'Good of you to come, Aunt,' Bob said as he drove her through the city traffic. 'I'm in a bit of a spot. Important medical experiment tonight and Eva's had to go to the South of France for a rest cure. Leaves me high and dry.'

'It should be,' Aunt Bertha agreed solemnly.

'Should be what?'

'Fine and dry. According to the forecast this morning.'

Bob did not try any more: the effect of shouting was too much. But once he got the placid old girl to the house he spent half an hour bellowing an explanation as to why he required her.

'And take no notice of our surgical

37

experiment,' he yelled. 'There'll be another doctor, a nurse, and a good-looking girl who needs treatment. Understand?'

'Perfectly. I'm not that hard of hearing, boy. I'll do all the domestic side, don't worry — and if you offer to pay for it I'll be insulted.'

Bob smiled in relief, mopped his face and found it was six o'clock. There was just time for a quick tea, a freshen-up, and then the fun would start — and at exactly seven o'clock there came the anticipated buzzing of the front door bell. Immediately Bob fled down the hall from the surgery and found three people waiting on the step — Boris Campbell, the irresistible Claire, and a teak-faced woman of late middle age, possessing a bosom of imposing dimensions.

'Here we come!' Campbell smiled, ushering the two women in ahead of him. 'Meet Nurse Addison, Bob. Nurse, this is Dr. Cranston.'

'Good evening, doctor.' The handshake was coldly formal and the glance even bleaker. 'From what I have heard from Dr. Campbell you are about to make a most unorthodox experiment.'

'You could call it that,' Bob agreed, then he quickly shook hands with the sunny-faced Claire.

'Everything okay, Claire?'

'Everything. Just give me time to get into the swimsuit and then I'm at your service.'

Nurse Addison's stone-grey eyes wandered from the girl to Bob, then across to Campbell. She remained immovable, her black hat rock-solid on her greying hair,

'I'll have my aunt show you to the spare bedroom,' Bob said. 'It's all fixed up for you. Pardon me a moment.'

He departed quickly, to return after a moment or two with Aunt Bertha. By dint of lung-bursting shouts he managed to make the position reasonably clear to her, and Claire was conducted upstairs, Aunt Bertha carrying the girl's suitcase.

'It is not clear to me,' Nurse Addison said, 'whether I am expected to remain indefinitely, or whether I am to assist only at the outset of the experiment.'

'At the moment I'm not sure myself,' Bob responded. 'I can tell you better when the experiment is under way.'

'Very good.' Satisfied, Nurse Addison removed her hat and coat, hung them purposefully on the hallstand, then turned. 'I am at your disposal, Dr. Cranston.'

'Thank you. This way to the surgery, please.'

Bob led the way down the hall and into the big surgery at the end of it. Nurse Addison followed him with the tread of a general, then when she surveyed the electrical instruments — far predominating the normal medical equipment — she looked puzzled.

'You have some remarkably queer apparatus here, Dr. Cranston.'

'Since the experiment I intend to conduct is completely off the normal track that is hardly to be wondered at. Has Dr. Campbell explained the process to you?'

'Yes indeed. Retardation of molecular activity by means of electrical processes, plunging the patient into deep unconsciousness bordering on pre-death coma. The dream of the medical world, Dr.

40

Cranston. Bloodless surgery!'

'Precisely.' Bob rubbed his hands in satisfaction. 'When a patient is in that condition any kind of surgery will be possible, there being no chance of blood loss. Afterwards, slow restoration to normal.'

'Quite, quite.' The starched bosom crackled like cellophane as the ex-matron prowled around the apparatus and studied it. Everything appeared to be centered in a transparent six-foot-long tube perched on a chromium cradle. To the ends and sides of it were fitted long, heavily-insulated cables which in turn led back to a large control panel in a corner of the surgery.

'I thought you would be interested,' Campbell commented, moving to the nurse's side. 'There is also the happy thought that when the experiment is completed we four — including Miss Baxter, I mean — will be hailed as the pioneers of this revolutionary form of surgery.'

'Quite, quite!' Nurse Addison's vocabulary seemed singularly limited to this observation, which she delivered with knife-edged sharpness. Then she came back to Bob as for about the hundredth time he checked the instruments. 'I am sure the Medical Council must look forward to the result of this experiment, Dr. Cranston!'

Bob smiled, looked under his eyes at Campbell — who was making hush-hush signals behind Nurse Addison's back — and then responded:

'Believe me, I shall await the Council's reaction with extreme interest.'

'Yes, yes, I'm sure. I was just wondering if — '

What the ex-matron was wondering was never discovered, for at that moment Claire entered the surgery, her shapely form buried at the moment beneath a silk dressing gown. Her loosened hair and merry smile made Bob clear his throat slightly, whilst Dr. Campbell looked down on her from his great height and beamed like a genial uncle. Only Nurse Addison remained unmoved. She glanced at the girl, then at her watch.

'Seven-fifteen,' she announced.

'Does that matter?' Campbell ventured, and the good woman's nostrils twitched.

'I was informed the experiment would commence at about seven-twenty and I am a stickler for punctuality.'

'Then let us commence!' Bob exclaimed fastening the bottom button of his overall. 'First, Claire, into the — '

'But what about the exoneration?' Claire interrupted. 'You want that, don't you?'

Bob snapped his fingers. 'Of course! I'd clean forgotten — ' He hurried to the bench, whisked a memo from the rack and laid it on the blotter. By the time he had the pen ready Claire was beside him, her hair radiating a faintly elusive aroma of roses. Bob decided inwardly that this experiment was going to be tougher to handle than he had imagined.

'Well?' Claire asked when he'd finished staring into space. 'What do I say?'

'Say? Oh — er — 'I, Claire Baxter, do hereby state — that I undertake to become — the patient of Doctors Cranston and Campbell entirely on my own free will — the objective being suspended animation. I hereby exonerate them wholly — and absolutely from any untoward accident or fatality that might occur . . . ' Then sign it and put the date.'

Claire nodded, dutifully did as she was told, and then handed the memo across.

'Splendid!' Bob nodded in satisfaction, folded it and put it into his overall pocket. 'Now, Claire, this is it. Still feel that you're up to it?'

'Of course! Why shouldn't I?'

'I just wondered, now we've reached the actual moment. If you want to back out I shan't think any the worse of you.'

'I never back out,' Claire said solemnly. 'Just tell me what to do and I'll do it.'

'This way, then — '

Bob led the way to the long, electrically connected tube. Nearby, Nurse Addison and Campbell stood waiting.

'What you have to do,' Bob said as Claire came to his side, 'is get into this tube and lie down on your back. After that, the end of the tube — where you enter — will be sealed up completely. There's an air-conditioning system inside the tube, which is thermostatically controlled to lessen in density as the temperature of your body drops. That is to say, the more you sink into the deep freeze of unconsciousness the less air you will require because your lungs will only be working at about three-quarters of normal. The idea of the tube is to seal you from external conditions that would prevent the successful deep freeze we're aiming at. Gradually, as you sink, the air will be removed from the tube until finally you will be in a partial vacuum, very close to that existing in interstellar space.'

Claire nodded, not in the least disturbed. Then she asked a question:

'Shall I dream?'

'Hard to say. Frankly, Claire, I don't know. Your own report on your sensations will be invaluable to medical science.'

'I see. Right then, here we go! Enter Claire Baxter, the 'Frozen Limit'!'

With that she slipped off the dressing gown and laid it on the nearby chair. Bob struggled to look professionally disinterested as he surveyed her perfect young figure in the tight-fitting swimsuit. Campbell lowered his brows so his eyes vanished, though there was little doubt which way they were looking. Nurse Addison waited, a starched pillar of strength.

'In here?' Claire asked cheerfully, vaulting with the ease of an athlete to the broad lip at the end of the tube.

'That's it,' Bob assented, and as she pushed her feet and legs into the opening he assisted by holding her shoulders and sliding her forward — until finally she was stretched at full length on the air-filled bed in the tube base.

'Everything all right?' he enquired.

'Everything's fine. Like being inside a space projectile I imagine.'

Bob adjusted the air pillow so her head was comfortable, then with a taut look on his generously ugly face he closed the end of the tube and spun the heavy clamps, which secured it. Within the tube Claire waggled her fingers in a signal. She said something, but her voice could not be heard.

'Now — ' Bob came across to where Nurse Addison and Campbell were standing. 'You, Nurse, had better keep a watch on this bank of registers here. They will show exactly the state of the patient as the freezing process continues. Heart-beats, respiration, blood pressure: they will all register.'

'I quite understand,' the ex-matron responded, surveying the meters. 'And if there is a divergence from what you consider is normal, what am I to do?'

'Inform me immediately. Variation of the current may be needed.'

'Very good. Incidentally, Doctor, although these registers are quite understandable, I have never seen any like them before.'

'They're specially made,' Bob explained. 'When the deep freeze is complete these are the only instruments in the world which will show the patient's condition. Normal medical instruments would be of no use in a case like this.'

'Quite, quite!'

'As for you, Boris — ' Bob turned to Campbell. 'I'd like you to keep an eye on that specially-devised voltmeter on the wall there. If it gets beyond the red line let me know right away. My whole attention will be fixed on the control of the current and I'll have no time to watch anything else.'

'Right!' Campbell moved into position and fixed his gaze on the — at present — motionless voltmeter needle on the zero mark.

'Which makes us ready,' Bob announced. 'It is exactly seven forty-five.'

He crossed over to the main switch-panel and closed the big knife-bladed make-and-break, which started up the generator. A deep hum, slowly rising to a whine, began to pervade the laboratory. Within the tube Claire still lay motionless on her air bed, though her eyes were clearly watching everything through the transparent wall. She smiled as Bob raised one hand with his fingers crossed —

Then he switched in the main power circuit that transferred the current to the curious filigree of wires netted around the tube. Here and there contact points glowed brightly and there was a steady crackling as electrical energy surged and died, surged and died.

'Heartbeats seventy,' came Nurse Addison's voice.

'Voltmeter fifteen hundred,' Campbell announced.

Bob made no comment. He knew the controls on the panel from long practice. The moment he had adjusted one of the maze of knobs he kept his eyes on the girl. He saw her slowly becoming drowsy. She yawned several times, waved to him limply, and then at last she made no movement at all. Bob slipped in an automatic control and moved to the case, scrutinizing the girl intently. There was a faint mist on the inner side of the tube and the girl herself was covered in millions of tiny droplets from the effect of condensation.

'Sixty-six,' Nurse Addison rapped out.

Bob returned to the controls. Campbell glanced at him and read no sign of dissatisfaction on the ugly face. Evidently everything was going as it should. The noise of the generator increased, and with this came a corresponding change in the needles of the various registers. In particular the thermometer registering the interior temperature of the tube began to show a decided drop.

In a matter of three minutes the register needle was down to 32 F. degrees and after that it began a steady crawl into the depths towards the normal Fahrenheit zero. Nor did it stop here. The register, specially devised for extreme below-zero temperatures, still continued the downward descent. Bob watched the meters intently and kept his hands on the controls; then he turned sharply at an exclamation from Nurse Addison.

'Dr. Cranston! The heartbeats are only registering sixteen to the minute! I insist that you stop! That girl cannot possibly live at such a slow pulse-rate.'

Bob glanced sharply. 'I'm the best judge of that, Nurse Addison. Even if the heartbeats only register two to the minute it will suffice.'

'Two! It's preposterous!'

Bob took no notice. He knew exactly what he was doing. And only when the temperature was minus 120 F. degrees did he switch off the power and turn to make a survey of the instruments Nurse Addison had been watching. She gave him a troubled look.

'I maintain, Dr. Cranston, that it is impossible to keep life going at such a low ebb. Look at that heart register. Barely three beats to the minute! And the blood pressure — !'

'Everything,' Bob said deliberately, 'is exactly as it should be. Whilst I appreciate your adherence to medical facts, Nurse, I must remind you that this experiment is right outside the field of ordinary medicine — hence the appearances are unusual. At the moment, Miss Baxter is in the coma caused by deep freezing. This is the vital part of the experiment. Consider, for instance, that some form of amputation were necessary upon Miss Baxter. All the surgeon would have to do would be to set up electrically-controlled instruments through that tube and so he could complete the amputation success-fully without drawing a drop of blood. At the moment, were we to make the test, we would find Miss Baxter's body as hard as a block or granite.'

Nurse Addison moved to the tube and looked within it upon the motionless girl. The condensation had gone now, and to the eye there was nothing to show the exceptionally low temperature of the girl's body. She looked dead-white and it was impossible to visually detect the extreme slowness of her breathing.

'With all respect to your professional skill, Dr. Cranston, I'd stake my reputation on this girl being dead!'

Bob smiled. 'You'd be wrong Nurse — quite wrong. What has happened is that the molecules of her body have been slowed down to the minimum. With that slowing down there comes coldness, since all energy of motion is purely molecular activity. That state of slow molecular movement will remain until the counteractive electrical energy is set in being, which will restore the molecular activity to normal.'

Nurse Addison sighed. 'Your scientific outlook is quite beyond me, Doctor Cranston.'

'That's common to all pioneers,' Campbell put in. 'It is because their methods are unorthodox that they are pioneers.'

There was a pause, a mutual study of

the recumbent, frozen Claire; then Nurse Addison stirred a little.

'What is required of me next, Dr. Cranston? Do you propose to restore the girl back to normal now you have proved your point?'

'I shall not restore her until the leading members of the Medical Council have seen her in her present condition. I have no idea when that will be, so in the meantime, Nurse, you are left with nothing to do.'

'I understand. You will require me, though, for the restoration, I assume?'

'Definitely,' Bob responded. 'The best thing I can do is get in touch with you the moment we're ready.'

'Quite, quite!' And upon that by now epic response the ex-matron departed from the surgery, far too active a woman to waste a single moment where she was not really needed. Bob saw her from the house and then came back into the surgery. He found Campbell half leaning on the tube, studying the girl within.

'Well, I think Nurse Addison served her purpose,' he said. 'She was a witness to the deep freeze and the method used, and that'll be a big help when we show the M.C. Otherwise we could have done without her.'

'Mmm,' Bob acknowledged, his brooding eyes on Claire.

'Considering what you have achieved you don't sound too cheerful!'

Bob smiled faintly. 'I'm satisfied enough, Boris, but this is only half the experiment, after all. When the whole thing is complete then I'll really start crowing. I think the best thing we can do is restore Claire this moment and get her reactions. Having done that we'll know that the whole business is satisfactory. With that established Claire can be frozen again — tomorrow maybe after she's had a good night's rest — and then we'll call in the Council.'

'All right with me. Why didn't you do it when Nurse Addison was here?'

'Didn't think of it. In any case we only needed her as a witness to the freezing. Claire's return to life doesn't need a witness, since Nurse Addison knows how she left her. Yes,' Bob decided, crossing to the control panel, 'we'll bring her back. It won't be as difficult as the first process. You don't need to watch the voltmeter. Keep your eye on the instruments Nurse Addison was watching.'

'Check!'

Bob closed the make-and-break and for the second time that evening the whine of the generator pervaded the surgery. When the meters showed it had pervaded the required pitch Bob transferred the current and then watched the needles flickering on their dials. After a moment or two a frown crossed his face. There did not appear to be any sign of current reversal as there normally should be when the molecular inactivity was being counteracted.

'What readings have you?' he demanded of Campbell.

'Nothing different so far. Just as they were.'

'Can't be! The moment the power started up there should have been signs of quickening heartbeats and — '

'There isn't. Come and look.'

Bob switched in the automatic control and then hurried to look at the meters.

Campbell had spoken the truth. The heartbeat register still showed three to the minute without the least sign of acceleration. Blood pressure reading was also unmoved.

'What's gone wrong?' A drawn look had come suddenly to Campbell's craggy face. 'Damnit, we put her into the freeze. Surely we ought to be able to pull her out?'

Bob did not answer. He started to prowl around desperately, checking plugs, ammeters, insulators, small transformers and even the wires themselves, but apparently there was nothing wrong. Indeed the master-meter showed that the generator's power was being transferred correctly to the tube, which in turn meant that the girl's molecular structure ought to be affected.

'Sure you reversed the system?' Campbell questioned, and Bob gave him an impatient look.

'Course I did — and have! If it were otherwise she'd be freezing still more. Be dead, in fact. No, it's not that. It's just that the current isn't having the reverse effect it should. Molecules should gather activity under the influence of this agitating electronic current — Hell, I'll have to figure it out.'

He left the automatic control in and then batted himself with panicky haste to find a piece of paper on which to figure. Finally he dragged a folded sheet from his overall pocket and worked on it quickly, taking readings from the meters. Campbell watched him anxiously.

'I don't get it!' Bob declared finally, balling up the paper and throwing it in the waste bin. 'The figuring checks to the last fraction. There's no conceivable reason why by this time Claire oughtn't to have come back to normal.'

He moved to the tube and looked at the girl, silent, well-moulded in her swimsuit, white as alabaster.

'Well, she hasn't.' Campbell leaned his forearms on the tube and stared within. Through the insulated glass there was no hint of the scaring cold existing within that circumscribed area.

'I'll try more power,' Bob decided, and went back to the switch panel — but though he stepped up the generator and tried various combinations of switches, he got no result whatever. Claire Baxter's heartbeats remained steady on three to the minute and her respiration was so slow the instruments barely registered it at all.

Finally Bob stopped the generator. Set-faced, utterly baffled, he turned and looked at Campbell. By now he was the more calm of the two, scowling thoughtfully until his eyes vanished.

'Anyway,' he said finally, 'she isn't dead. The instruments prove it.'

'What consolation is that — either to her or to us? We just daren't show her to the M.C. when we can't revive her. And if we never revive her, what happens?'

'That's thinking on the morbid side, Bob. Doesn't do!'

Bob rubbed the back of his neck in bewilderment. He looked again at Claire. She might have been beautifully modeled wax. Odd thing, too — the main veins showed against her white skin in thin blue tracery. She was the nearest thing to a corpse that could be imagined.

'Must be the electrical power,' Campbell decided at length. 'Let's check it over. You compare everything with your wiring diagram and I'll see that all connections are okay.'

'Right!' Bob was glad enough to do anything. This was the most alarming happening he had ever known. Not for an instant had he thought revival might misfire. From the safe he brought the wiring diagram and for a solid two hours after that he and Campbell checked everything they could find, went right through the whole complicated circuit — and found everything was just as it should be.

'Mmm,' Campbell observed as they hit up against this stone wall. 'Damned odd! Do you suppose the mains power might be down? Would that caused anything unusual?'

'Might, but it's unlikely.' Bob crossed to the switch panel and snapped on the subsidiary meter, which gave him the mains line reading. It was perfectly normal: indeed slightly up if anything, since it was night time.

'Beyond me,' Campbell confessed. 'We've a lot of hard thinking to do to get this lot straight. Not that I can do very much since I didn't invent the apparatus in the first place.'

'It isn't the apparatus!' Bob swung and faced him urgently. 'Everything checks. Therefore the fault is in Claire herself, or rather the molecules that make up her body. By all the laws of electronics and mathematics the energy I'm using ought to activate the molecules back to normal speed. But it just doesn't happen!'

'What's the difference between the energy you used to create the deep freeze and the one you're using for reversal — or trying to?'

'The difference lies in the frequency. To create the deep freeze the frequency in electronic volts registers around twenty-eight hundred, which is sufficient to produce an outwardly spreading dampening wave, which reacts on the electrical charges of the molecules themselves. It doesn't cancel out those charges, otherwise actual dissolution would result. Instead it slows up the speed with which the molecules are moving — creates an electrical brake as it were — and deep freeze results as the molecules slow down.'

'Uh-huh. And that condition remains even when the 'braking' effect is removed?'

'Yes, but to explain why that happens is rather involved.' Bob thought for a moment, then: 'Look at it this way: If a balloon is coming towards you and you slap it away it naturally recoils from the blow. Now at the peak of its backward movement it halts for a split second, reaching what is technically called the apex of shock. Then it begins to drift again. Imagine that on the microscopic scale applied to molecules and you will see that the braking effect which slowed them down remains for a time after the 'shock' of the braking has been removed — '

'Then they'll gradually start to return to normal?'

'Yes — but not for many years.'

'Years!' Campbell started in alarm. 'Why years? A balloon which is hit doesn't take years to move again — '

'We can't carry the analogy that far,'

Bob said quietly. 'With molecules we enter the dimension of Time. To a molecule, one second might be a year of our standard time. That is caused by the stupendous difference in sizes and the relativity theory. The smaller one gets the greater the discrepancy with what we call normal time. The 'shock' apex of a molecule might — in our time measure — be anything from one to ten years before any visible movement takes place. By visible I mean capable of being registered, since we obviously can never see a molecule. My 'reversal' frequency as I call it is simply a weak boosting charge of electricity which should jolt the molecules into getting on the move again. Rather in the way one shunting wagon can set a whole line of them on the move. But it hasn't worked out!'

'I wonder,' Campbell said slowly, 'if you have made the ghastly mistake of not including the time factor in your calculations?'

Bob frowned. 'How do you mean? I've allowed for everything!'

'Are you sure? I'm looking at it as a

kind of independent observer, and this is what I see: that the molecules of Claire were slowed down from the standpoint of Now — normal time. Right?'

'If you mean that we began the retardation from the aspect of NOW, yes we did.'

'Okay then. By retarding them we produced, you say a shock apex, which may last — to the molecule — anything from one to ten of our years. If that be so, how can a reversal current reach to those molecules immediately? Doesn't it mean that you have brought a Time-factor into it, produced a shock retardation which will take years to expend itself, and therefore the molecules are right out of electrical reach?'

'My God!' Bob whispered, staring in front of him. 'The time factor! Yes, it does enter into it. It enters into all mathematical formulae that deal with the infinitely small. By the very act of producing a shock we brought in the dimension of Time and put the molecules ten years out of reach. Then, or sooner, the shock apex will have passed and the normal balance will slowly restore.'

'That,' Campbell said slowly, 'is the way it looks.'

Silence. The surgery door clicked suddenly, but because it was bolted nobody came in. Bob moved to it and pulled back the catch. Aunt Bertha was outside.

'It's nearly half past ten,' she announced. 'Would you and Dr. Campbell care for supper? I fixed it all up for you.'

'You have?' Bob gave a moody glance. 'Oh, I don't think we can be bothered eating, Aunt — '

'Who can't?' Campbell demanded. 'Speak for yourself, man! If we starve ourselves we'll get nowhere. We can think just as well eating as stewing in here.'

'No,' Aunt Bertha said gently. 'It isn't stew, Dr. Campbell. I've just fixed up sandwiches, and — '

'Right, Aunt,' Bob interrupted, forcing a smile. 'And thanks. We'll come right away.'

Pondering, he led the way out of the surgery with Campbell close beside him. Aunt Bertha departed into the kitchen regions, and presently reappeared in the lounge with steaming coffee; then she left the two men to their own devices.

'Of course,' Bob said at length, when the coffee had somewhat cheered him, 'it is only a theory. About the Time-factor, I mean.'

'I agree. We might be off the beam, but at least it's one possible explanation of the failure to revive Claire.'

Bob reflected, emphasizing his thoughts by stabbing the air with his coffee spoon.

'For the original retardation I used a very powerful electrical field; and for the reversal a comparatively weak booster charge. Wonder if it's too weak?' But he immediately corrected himself by shaking his head. 'No, that's not it. I tried varying doses, none of them very strong, certainly, but we still got no result.'

'The pity is that we have no way of finding out if the charge is being received by Claire. Or have we?'

'No way, except by the instruments. Mmm, come to think of it, they didn't register!' Bob frowned. 'But damnit, it's inconceivable that the current isn't being received by Claire. She got it on the retardation frequency, so why not on the reverse? Nothing was altered. Nothing broke down.'

'True.'

Silence, and the munching of the sandwiches. Then Campbell gave a sigh.

'Maybe we'll sort it out after a night's sleep. Meantime, let's look at the other aspect. How are we going to explain our failure to produce a revival? Nurse Addison will naturally want to know what's going on. So far she hasn't guessed that the M.C. have frowned on you. If we don't show something concrete quickly she's the sort of woman who'll go straight to the M.C. President and report that there's something fishy. Then the fat will be in the fire with a vengeance!'

'Yes.' Bob rubbed his chin. 'Have to fob her off somehow until we get things straight. And get them straight we must! Consider the position! Claire frozen there in the surgery and she can't be moved — Lord, even if the heavens fall we've got to revive her. My wife will come back eventually and you know the dim view she takes of my experiments. When she sees a girl like Claire lying there — '

Campbell grinned faintly, and Bob gave him a sour glance.

'All very well for you!'

'Don't be too sure! My ambition is to marry Claire, not to see her lying year after year like frozen mutton. Anyhow, we'll have to think it out, Bob, and — '

Aunt Bertha suddenly appeared, toddling in cheerfully with a waste bin in her hand.

'Anything more, gentlemen?' She looked at them both.

'No, Aunt, you've done a grand job.' Bob's eyes traveled in wonder to the waste bin. It belonged to the surgery. 'What are you doing with that, Auntie?'

'Fat?' She frowned. 'I know I'm a little overweight, but — '

'That!' Bob pointed to the bin. 'Why are you carting it about? The char will do all the cleaning when she comes.'

'Oh!' Auntie comprehended. 'I just cleaned up the surgery for you, boy. It looked dreadfully untidy. If there's nothing more I'll go to bed.'

Bob smiled and nodded to save the strain on his voice and, satisfied, Aunt Bertha departed. It was the signal for Campbell to glance at his watch.

'I'd better be on the move, too — '

'Stay here if you like. The spare bedroom's there even though it was meant for Claire. Pair of my pyjamas will fit you.'

'Done!'

3

Eva Returns

The following morning the situation concerning Claire was in no way clarified, and certainly a night's sleep had not served in any way to clarify the ideas of the two men. For that matter Bob had hardly slept at all. At breakfast, provided by the undisturbed Aunt Bertha, he looked particularly bleary-eyed. Campbell, on the contrary, was fairly complacent. By and large, of course, he had not nearly so much on his mind as Bob, even though he was still obviously resenting the fact that his intended fiancée was frozen solid.

'You've no ideas at all, then?' Campbell questioned when they had come to the end of the eggs and bacon and marmalade that lay before them.

'Nothing concrete anyway. I have considered the possibility of telling the M.C. what a mess I've made of things

69

and leaving it to them to find a scientist somewhere who can think more clearly on this business than I can.'

'Not likely!' Campbell shook his head vigorously. 'That's the very last thing you must do. We've got to sort it out ourselves. If it takes a long time it can't be helped. Claire is quite safe as long as she remains frozen and the heartbeats don't get any slower.'

'One to ten years!' Bob groaned. 'Damnit, man, it's an unthinkable possibility — '

Campbell carefully put some marmalade on his toast. 'Y'know, Bob, I keep thinking about something, though as yet I haven't pinned down where it comes in. It's this: For the original freezing you used a powerful — underline powerful — electric frequency, and for the restoration a weak booster charge. Underline weak.'

'Underline what you like, but I'm sure there's something important in the fact that only a weak charge was used for the restoration. The very weakness of it may account for its failure.'

Bob gave a dubious glance. 'I can't somehow see the point of that. My investigation is going to be along the line of molecular resistance and see if I can't find a way to defeat the time lag.'

'If it is that!'

'I thought we'd agreed upon it?'

'As a theory, yes — but we've nothing to back it up. There are other theories, too, such as the one I've just mentioned. They are all equally possible. Don't give up hope too soon. I'm going to do plenty of thinking whilst I'm on my rounds today.'

Bob gave a start. For the moment he had completely overlooked that there was such a thing as the normal work-a-day world, and that he too had an insignificant number of patients to attend to.

'You'll come back again soon as you're free, I suppose?'

'Certainly, if you wish it — though I can't see any purpose in just moping around hoping for the best. We can't move until we have something definite —'

Which was true enough — and Campbell had nothing further to add to

71

this, either. After he had completed his breakfast he went to take a further look at the motionless Claire — and then he went back on his way. Bob was left moodily studying the perfect figure in the tube and wondering if he ought to devise some means of injection. In every way he was at sea, for he had never calculated on a protracted coma, and now it had come about he was not sure whether nourishment was required or not. Presumably it was, for even to have heartbeats the girl was consuming a certain amount of energy, which required replacement.

It was the buzzing of the telephone that aroused Bob from his meditations. He crossed the surgery into the hall, knowing that Aunt Bertha, busy in the domestic regions, would never hear the instrument. There was even the astonishing possibility that it might be a patient — or a prospective one.

'Doctor Cranston speaking,' Bob said morosely, and waited.

'You sound wonderfully cheerful, Bob! What's the matter? Missing wee wifey?'

Bob came back to earth with a bump. It

was unquestionably Eva talking, the line crystal clear even though it was from the South of France.

'Eva darling! Hello, there! Nice to hear your voice! How are you?'

'Fine! Couldn't be better!'

'Splendid! Then my prescription for a cure is working?'

'More than that, it's worked. I'm coming home this evening.'

'Eh?' Bob stared before him, wrestling with disturbing possibilities. 'Coming home, did you say? But you mustn't do that yet: you're not fit. You've hardly spent any time relaxing as yet.'

'Judging from what Sir Gerald Warburton has to say I've no need to. He's here, you know — also on a holiday, but when I asked him specially and turned on the charm he took time out to give me a work-over.'

'Oh, he did!' Bob frowned ominously to himself. Sir Gerald Warburton, as he well knew, was a specialist in nervous troubles. Damn the man! He would have to be in the same place as Eva at the most inopportune time.

'He says I'm in perfect condition,' Eva resumed blithely. 'I told him that you thought you'd caught the trouble just in time, and in that he concurred. He seemed a bit vague, though, as to what the trouble might have been.'

'Mmm.'

'Did you say something, dear?'

'No — no. Maybe the line — Just the same, I don't think you ought to come home.'

'But why on earth not? It's costing a terrible lot to keep me here. Besides I'm happier beside you. I'm taking the six o'clock plane. I ought to be beside you again some time before midnight. All the news then.'

'But, Eva — '

'Bye, dear. Time's up.' And the line clicked.

Bob put the phone back slowly, a look of supreme stupidity momentarily on his face. He had not the vaguest idea what he ought to do next. He had sent Ella packing, for at least another three weeks; inscrutable Aunt Bertha was prowling around in her place; and then there was the immovable and highly delectable Claire in the surgery.

'Whew!' Bob muttered, mopping his face. 'This is going to be a tough one. I might be able to scramble over an explanation concerning Ella, but Claire is a different proposition entirely.'

The front door bell rang and, not expecting it, Bob jumped violently. Almost with a snarl he charged to the door and whipped it open. On the step Nurse Addison stood looking at him in cold impartiality.

'Good morning, doctor.' She stepped into the hall with a firm tread.

'Good morning, nurse.' Bob's politeness had a curiously strangled quality.

'I assume,' Nurse Addison said, 'that you have been so busy with Miss Baxter and the various details connected with the demonstration before the Medical Council that you forgot to advise me to come. So here I am.'

'Er — yes, so I see. Won't you come into the lounge?'

'Wouldn't it be more to the point if I went into the surgery? I am here to work, doctor, not pay a social call.'

'Yes, I know, but — Well, fact of the matter is, I'm working on a dossier of Miss Baxter's case. As you will understand that takes a little time.'

'Quite, quite!'

'And for that reason I am not ready yet to present my demonstration to the Council. It may be — ' Bob moved a hand airily. 'Oh, a couple of weeks.'

Nurse Addison stared. 'A couple of weeks?'

'I'm afraid so. Great deal of intricate work involved in the dossier.'

'I can understand that, but what happens to Miss Baxter in the meantime? Or have you revived her?'

'Er — yes, indeed.' Bob smiled blandly, feeling this lie would make things easier. 'We revived her and then put her to sleep again. All very interesting.'

The cold eyes stared again, fishlike and faintly accusative.

'Tell me, doctor, wouldn't it have been more sensible — and indeed more comfortable for Miss Baxter — if you had allowed her to stay revived until your dossier is complete?'

'Couldn't be done,' Bob answered. 'One cannot study the reactions of an unconscious person when they're awake. That is surely logic?'

'Quite, quite, but — '

'If you would be so good, Nurse, I'll send for you when I need you, just as I promised. In this case I am afraid you have somewhat anticipated the event.'

'More than anticipated, I fancy. It has come, gone, and even started again. You will forgive me remarking, doctor, that I find your experiment a most unusual one?'

'Quite! I — I mean, of course. After all, unorthodox experiments demand unorthodox measures.'

Bob already had the front door open and he hoped the look on the ex-matron's face did not presage dangerous action of some kind. She left the house without speaking a word, hat firmly on the top of her head, her walk to the gate full of grim resolution.

'Hell!' Bob muttered, shutting the front door. 'This gets tougher with every second that passes — '

He crossed to the telephone, snatched it up and dialed quickly. A sing-song voice answered him.

'Dr. Campbell there? This is urgent — Dr. Cranston speaking.'

'Sorry, doctor. Dr. Campbell won't be back yet awhile: he's on his rounds.'

'Ask him to call me the moment he gets back, please. Stress that it is most urgent.'

'Very well, doctor.'

Muttering to himself Bob went back into the surgery, surveyed the motionless girl and scratched his head helplessly, and then shivered. The surgery was cold. In fact the whole house was cold. Usually Ella kept things at a comfortable temperature by the use of the central heating furnace in the small basement, but evidently Aunt Bertha was not up to these things.

Struggling against an outburst of sheer bad temper Bob went in search of Aunt Bertha and found her making the beds. He forced a genial smile.

'Know anything about tending a central heating furnace, Aunt?'

She turned and shook her head. 'They

give me indigestion. Repeat something awful.'

'Eh?' Bob had enough on his mind without playing games. He raised his voice to the required bellow.

'Heating furnace! Can you look after it?'

'Furnace? I thought you said 'eating turnips.' Where is it? I'll — '

'I can light it and you keep it going later if you will, please. It's in the basement, next door to the coal cellar.'

Aunt, holding her hand to her ear, gave a nod. 'I'll tell you something, boy — this house is dreadful cold. As for that young woman in her bathing suit she looks as if she could do with a furnace to herself. I could swear I saw frost on her — real frost! — when I tidied up last night.'

'No doubt you did. She is undergoing a medical treatment known as suspended animation and deep freeze. It will make operations much — ' Bob paused, a faraway look suddenly coming into his eyes. 'Furnace to herself, didn't you say?'

Aunt nodded, though she had not the remotest idea what Bob was talking about. He had unconsciously lowered his voice as a thought had evidently struck him.

'Now I wonder — ' Bob wandered out of the bedroom absently and returned to the surgery. Uppermost in his mind was the remark Aunt Bertha had made — 'she looks as if she could do with a furnace to herself!'

'Possible,' Bob muttered. 'After all, external application of heat is only another way of producing increased activity of the molecules. If I were to take her into the furnace cellar, free of the tube, would she die or would she thaw out?'

This was something he could not answer, and back of his mind the whole idea seemed a dreadful risk. Then, as he was trying to make his mind up, the telephone rang. He glanced, frowned, and hurried into the hall.

'What this time?' came the voice of Campbell as Bob raised the phone. 'I got back sooner than I expected and found your message waiting. Has Claire recovered?'

'No, there's no change. The crisis is that the wife is coming home again and she'll be here by midnight. What to do with Claire is a problem.'

'Why the devil can't you tell your wife what you're trying to do?'

'I can, of course, but I shudder to think what her reaction may be. For one thing I told her you were bringing a man for treatment, and as I've said already she's no faith in my experiments. What would you think if you returned to behold a half-clad and very pretty girl laid out in a tube?'

'I'm not your wife so I can't tell you. Well, what's to be done?'

'I was wondering about the possibility of putting Claire in the furnace cellar, removing her from the tube. It might have the effect of starting her molecules going again. Natural warmth as opposed to electrical energy. Same thing when you boil it down.'

'Risky,' Campbell commented after a pause. 'She might fall to pieces or something. I don't like it. We'd better still keep working on the scientific angle.'

'We'll keep doing that, naturally, but in the meantime I have the wife to consider. Down in the cellar Claire isn't likely to be discovered. Eva never bothers with the furnace; that's Ella's job. And whilst Ella is away I'll deal with it, or my harmless old aunt will — '

'Just the same,' Campbell broke in, 'I don't think we ought to leave Claire down in the cellar indefinitely. Not in your cellar anyhow. Tell you what, I've a photographer friend who's a pretty large basement he might be willing to loan. I'll pop over and see him and let you know the result. We might be able to wangle Claire out of your house somehow. I can always fix an ambulance job in which to take her — tube and all. Be playing havoc with the regulations, but needs must sometimes.'

'Okay,' Bob said in relief. 'Ring me back when you've got something. Meantime I'll transport Claire below — I won't take her from the tube: might be too dangerous. It means that the warmth won't do her any good because of the tube's insulation, but at least she won't be on view when — and if — Eva wanders into the surgery as she sometimes does.'

On that Campbell rang off and Bob returned to the surgery. He spent a few moments uncoupling the various cables, none of which were necessary unless he were actually using the electric energy, the tube maintaining the temperature at which it had arrived, because of the insulating system. With this done he began to raise the tube from its supports, only to desist as he realized the job was too much for him single-handed.

Immediately he went in search of Aunt Bertha. Middle-aged though she was she was still strong enough. Thanks to her at the opposite end of the tube it was gradually transported down into the furnace-basement and laid on the door until the cradle could be fixed up.

'One thing I want you to understand, Aunt,' Bob shouted as he struggled to get the cradle in position. 'Eva is not to know about this tube being down here, and even less about the girl inside it. Not that there's anything 'peculiar,' mind you, only these medical experiments are always strictly hush-hush.'

Aunt nodded and gave a sly smile. 'That's all right, boy. I've been young myself.'

How this remark was supposed to be taken Bob did not quite know. He finished arranging the cradle and then, again with Aunt's help, got the tube securely fixed on to it. After which Aunt returned above, muttering something to herself. Bob glared after her.

'Been young myself indeed! What the blazes sort of a game does she think this is, I wonder?'

He would probably have been surprised had he known. Since he did not he abandoned thinking about the matter and instead turned his attention to lighting the furnace fire. And it was also about this time that Nurse Addison was seated in the private office of the President of the Medical Council. From the look of her she was in her most belligerent mood.

'Frankly, Sir James, I feel I should bring to your notice a rather remarkable set of circumstances connected with young Dr. Robert Cranston. Not that everything isn't above board — I wouldn't go so far as to suggest otherwise — but I do feel there is something peculiar.'

'Indeed?' Sir James was a solid, grey-haired man, eminent in the medical world. 'Dr. Cranston has always impressed the Council as being quite a go-ahead young doctor. A trifle given to scientific theorizing, perhaps, but nothing more.'

'That is the point. It is this experiment in deep freezing that bothers me. Naturally you will be expecting a demonstration as quickly as possible, but apparently there is going to be some delay whilst Dr. Cranston completes his dossier afterwards.'

'Demonstration?' Sir James's eyes sharpened. 'What demonstration?'

'But — but surely you know? Dr. Cranston would never dare to perform a dangerous, revolutionary experiment without the consent of the Council. Why, he would jeopardize his practice.'

'Definitely he would!' The presidential jaw was beginning to jut. 'This is becoming a serious matter, Nurse, and you are to be congratulated for bringing it to my notice. For your information, Dr. Cranston did apply for permission to make a suspended animation experiment on a volunteer, but we refused to allow it on account of the danger involved. You don't mean to tell me — '

'But I do!' The ex-matron stared in horror. 'Great heavens, can it be, then, that I have been inveigled by Dr. Campbell into an illegal experiment, one upon which the Council has placed its veto?'

'Campbell? Not Boris Campbell, surely? He's one of the cleverest young doctors on the register. I thought you said Dr. Cranston?'

'They're both in it together, and it was Dr. Campbell who asked me to take part. I did so and saw this young woman — a highly attractive one, I might add — put into a state of deep unconsciousness by freezing process, but I did not see her revived.'

'Then what?' Sir James asked ominously.

'I called this morning — ' and with

noticeable venom Nurse Addison went into a long explanation.

'All very peculiar,' Sir James mused. 'On the face of it, it would appear that Dr. Cranston does not wish the young woman to be seen until he has written his dossier, and throughout all that time he unlawfully has this young woman plunged into deep unconsciousness.'

'That would appear to be the situation, sir.'

'Naturally,' Sir James said, 'we must take action.'

'Quite, quite!'

Silence whilst the great man thought it out. Then at length he cleared his throat pontifically.

'We must, of course, exercise extreme caution, Nurse. I believe every word, I assure you, but we have to be guarded that we do not leap to conclusions.'

Nurse Addison's nostrils twitched. 'It would appear to me, sir, that there is only one conclusion which can be reached — namely, that Doctors Campbell and Cranston are acting contrary to the edict of the Medical Council.'

'True; but I may as well tell you that I was not exactly in accord with the Council's somewhat arbitrary decision. The reason for the veto was — I tell you in confidence — not so much to protect a possible volunteer as to safeguard certain famous surgeons who shall be nameless. They saw in this new development of almost automatic, bloodless surgery, a distinct threat to their own skill — I am more broad-minded.'

'What am I to understand from that?' Nurse Addison asked bleakly.

'You are to understand that progress in medical or any other science is not possible without somebody flouting all the regulations and taking the plunge. That, apparently, is what these two young doctors have done — and I don't altogether blame them. They might even pull the thing off. Indeed, from what you tell me, they apparently have done so. That, I say, is my personal opinion. As the Council President I am supposed to act.'

'No doubt of it,' the ex-matron said flatly.

'If, though, this experiment is a

successful one, and we do indeed stand on the brink of a new era of medical wizardry then we do not wish to spoil it. There are certain occasions when it is advantageous to turn a blind eye to regulations. This may be one of those times.'

'Which means you suggest nothing should be done? Really, Mr. President, I cannot believe that you — '

'I didn't say that. I said we must proceed with caution, and that is where you can help.'

Nurse Addison smirked and gave a complacent little wriggle. To be thus delegated as ambassador — or spy — to the Council was jam indeed.

'I would suggest you proceed as though nothing has happened,' the President continued, 'but make a point of calling yet again on Dr. Cranston when he is not expecting you. Pin him down to a deadline for his dossier, and if you can do so get a look at the body of this young woman. We have got to establish that he really has revived her after putting her to sleep. If he has not, then the matter becomes grave. If he has, and you have incontestable proof of it, then I shall do my utmost to smooth the way to a waiving of the regulations. Great thinkers in the advancement of medical science are rare — '

Upon which magnificent statement the President left it clear that the interview was over, and the ex-matron took her departure. Meantime, Bob Cranston — quite unaware: that sundry plans had been drafted against him — had at last got the furnace fire going and returned upstairs. It dawned upon him that by rights he ought to make the rounds of certain of his more urgent patients then he shook his head. Nothing so badly the matter with any of them that they couldn't wait for another day. He had too many other matters to concentrate upon —

Then again the telephone rang. It was Campbell's irritatingly cheerful voice at the other end of the line.

'I fixed it!' he announced. 'Lovely basement for as long as we want. Power laid on too if we decide to make further experiments in revival.'

'If we do! Damnit, man, it's essential!'

'Yes, but I mean if natural processes don't somehow reassert themselves. Anyway, it seems to me it's only a matter of fixing up when I can get an ambulance.'

'Sooner the better whilst the coast's clear. Let's see — ' Bob glanced at his watch. 'It's half past eleven. How about noon? Most people will be thinking of lunch instead of studying what we're doing.'

'Noon it shall be! Rely on it.'

And noon it was. Exactly upon twelve a private ambulance drew up outside the gateway of Bob's home. Not that the neighbors, ever inquisitive, saw anything extraordinary about this. An ambulance outside a doctor's residence could be considered the most natural thing in the world. Campbell himself had evidently traveled with it, for he alighted quickly and came hurrying up the front path.

Bob opened the door to him and motioned quickly. 'In the basement. You'll have to give me a hand.'

Together they descended the basement

steps. Down here the heating furnace was going full blast, but the girl in the tube was still coated with that curious fine glaze of deadly cold. Campbell looked at her, unable to prevent the fascination that came into his expression.

'If only we could revive her as thoroughly as we've put her out, Bob!'

'Never mind that: give me a hand to move this tube. It's pretty heavy. Old Aunt Bertha nearly gave herself palpitation giving me a hand — '

'You down there, Robert?' demanded a voice, which clearly belonged to Aunt Bertha herself.

'Now what?' Bob groaned, wheezing as with Campbell he lowered the tube to the floor. 'Yes, Aunt, I'm here!' he bawled. 'Do you want me?'

'There's a nurse to see you. You'd better come.'

Nothing more than that, as though it were the easiest thing in the world. But to Bob it sounded like a knell of doom.

'Nurse?' Campbell repeated, starting. 'Not Nurse Addison?'

'Must be. I don't know any other nurse

who'd call — I'll have to fob her off somehow. Wait here for me and throw up a smoke screen or something if she tries to come down here.'

Bob fled for the stairs and arrived somewhat disheveled and furnace-dirty in the hall. Nurse Addison, her great bosom bulging magnificently, gave him a cold glance.

'I trust I haven't interrupted anything?' she enquired, and dealt a significant glance towards the ambulance visible through the open front door.

'No, no — of course not,' Bob responded hurriedly, and she looked surprised.

'I had rather thought, seeing the ambulance there — '

'May I ask what you want?' Bob recovered his dignity with some effort, unconscious of the fact that the effect was spoiled because of the amount of dirt on his face. 'I thought I made it quite clear that I would send for you when you were needed. That moment has not yet arrived.'

'Possibly not, Dr. Cranston, but it

occurred to me that since this dossier of yours is taking up so much of your time I'd be failing in my duty if I didn't make an effort to help you. I am willing to look after the professional side of your practice whilst you concentrate on the dossier. That way, things can be speeded up. I don't want the Medical Council to become tired of waiting for you to demonstrate.'

'I cannot imagine anything more unlikely than that,' Bob murmured.

'I beg your pardon, doctor?'

'Er — just thinking out loud, nurse. Honestly, there is nothing you can do to help.'

Nurse Addison compressed her thin lips. 'Forgive me, doctor, but I find that hard to believe. Surely I can be of help concerning the patient you are now having removed in that ambulance?'

'Patient? Oh, I see what you mean.' Bob smiled uncomfortably. 'Matter of fact, the ambulance has nothing to do with the patient. It just happened to be coming this way and a fellow doctor friend of mine decided to use it to save time. Er — his own car has broken down.'

This facer made the ex-matron blink somewhat. Never in her professional career had she heard of such strangely loose conduct by men of an honoured calling.

'I gather then that there is nothing I can do. Might I ask how Miss Baxter is faring?'

'No change. Still unconscious — but of course I can restore her any moment I choose.'

'Would I be transgressing if I had a look at her?'

'Not transgressing,' Bob responded warily, 'but it would be somewhat inconvenient. The doctor who arrived in the ambulance is in the surgery, waiting for me to conduct a most important discussion.'

'I see.' Nurse Addison's nostrils dilated slightly. 'Pardon my saying it, doctor, but I was not aware you had transferred your surgery to the basement!'

Bob blinked and watched her stalk outside again, every line of her movements typifying her outraged dignity. She spared a second to survey the ambulance and deliver what was probably a snort of disgust, then she strode on her way.

'Interfering old baggage,' Bob muttered, and returned into the cellar where Campbell was standing beside the tube and mopping his face in the heat from the furnace.

'Well, was it Nurse Addison?' he demanded.

'Yes — and I don't think I extricated myself very well either. Take it from me, Boris, there's going to be trouble with that woman before we're finished! She's as suspicious as hell as it is.'

'Just as long as she can't prove anything — ' Campbell paused and gave a start. 'The ambulance! She must have seen it! Did she make any comment?'

'She did, yes, and I handed out what must have sounded the most idiotic excuse ever! I said a doctor friend of mine had come in it because his car had broken down.'

'You didn't mention my name, I hope!'

'No — ' Bob aroused himself from disturbing speculations. 'Anyway, let's finish this confounded job. Grab your end — '

Campbell shook his head slowly. 'I don't think we should, Bob. Now that old buzzard of an Addison is suspicious she'll probably watch the house to see who leaves. If she saw us two carrying out this tube, no matter how much we wrap it up to try and disguise it, I'll gamble she'd turn up again and start asking awkward questions.'

'Mmm — maybe you're right. What do we do then? I've got to be rid of Claire before the wife comes home.'

Campbell reflected. 'Best thing is for me to stay here until nightfall, which fortunately is pretty early at this time of year. You can nip out and tell the ambulance driver to come back at, say, seven this evening. Under cover of darkness we can take a chance. If Nurse Addison is still watching then she won't be able to see much, anyway, and certainly she won't be able to identify me. I'm thinking about my practice old man. The M.C. doesn't take kindly to doctors who behave oddly. You are deliberately taking a gamble to prove your case, but I'm not.'

'Right,' Bob agreed after thinking swiftly. 'We'll see how that angle works. I'll tell the ambulance driver right away.'

4

Suspicion Deepens

The afternoon passed uneventfully, Campbell keeping in touch with his home by telephone in case some emergency demanded his services. To his profound relief nothing unusual was demanded, and finally seven o'clock arrived and the ambulance returned. Immediately Bob took what appeared to be a casual survey of the street outside, not particularly brilliantly illuminated, and decided that everything was at last ripe for action.

'We can do it in five minutes,' Campbell said, striding to the basement door in the hall. 'Let's get busy — '

They hurried below, leaving both the front and basement door open in readiness for a quick 'getaway' with the frozen girl. It was when they were half way up the basement stairs, however, struggling with the heavy tube between them, that Bob suddenly paused.

'Now what?' Campbell panted, taking the full load of the tube on his shoulders. 'Hurry up, can't you?'

'I can hear something! A woman's voice — and there was a squeak like brakes — Hang on to the tube for a second.'

Bob perched his own end of the tube on the basement steps and then squirmed under it and down into the cellar. In two strides he had reached the grating down which boiler fuel was shot. Very cautiously he drew aside the clamp, lifted the grating carefully and peered in the direction of the front gate. He gave a gulp. The ambulance was still there, but so was a taxi — and beside the taxi stood a young woman in a fur coat and a taxi driver carrying a suitcase. They began to come up the drive.

Bob lowered the grating instantly and fled back to the basement stairs.

'Bob, for the love of Mike!' Campbell complained. 'I'm just breaking off at the ankles carrying this weight — '

'The wife!' Bob whispered tautly. 'Put

the tube back! Sssh! Not a sound.'

'Your wife! But I thought she said midnight — '

'She did. Must have caught an earlier plane — Quickly, man!'

Wheezing with effort and doing their best to make no noise they carried the tube back once more to the trestle beside the furnace. They had hardly done so before Eva's voice floated down to them.

'Bob! Where are you, dear? I'm back again — '

'You're telling me,' Bob muttered, and turned a smudged face to Campbell. 'Work this one out for yourself, Boris. Escape as best you can. What we do now I just don't know!'

'I do. I'll escape as best I can and we'll move Claire during the night sometime. Tell you what I'll do: I'll ring you up and fix the most suitable time — have to square it with my photographer friend because of the lateness of the hour. Might as well have some sort of a signal so you'll know it's me when I arrive. A tune of some kind. I'll think of one by the time I phone.'

'Fair enough — '

'Bob! Where on earth are you?' The demand from above had now become impatient. Immediately Bob pulled himself together, flattened his hair quickly with his hand and then went in swift silence up the basement steps.

He found Eva with her back turned, gazing wonderingly about her.

'Why, darling!' Bob hurried forward and caught her in his arms, taking care to urge her into the lounge at the same time. 'I didn't expect you before midnight at least — '

'No; I managed it earlier.' Eva's small-featured face was vaguely suspicious. 'Where did you pop from, anyway? The surgery?'

'Er — no. The basement. I've been getting the furnace going properly. Aunt Bertha doesn't properly understand the technique, I'm afraid.'

Bob saw to it that Eva sat down on the settee, then he closed the lounge door to give Campbell a chance to escape the house.

'I've already noticed that Aunt Bertha's

here,' Eva said, 'and I can't think why! What's happened to Ella?'

'Trouble at home, I'm afraid.' Bob's face became serious. 'Her father desperately ill — or something. Anyway, I told her she could take a month to get things straight. Meanwhile I had Aunt Bertha take over the domestic side.'

'I see. Pity she's so deaf.'

Bob sat down on the settee and put his arm about Eva's shoulders. 'And you, sweetheart? From what you said over the phone I gather you're quite recovered?'

'Yes — I suppose so.' Eva looked puzzled. 'Matter of fact, Sir Gerald Warburton found it pretty difficult to understand what was supposed to have been the matter with me. He said after his overhaul that he'd seen few young women so fit.'

'Oh? Well, I simply stated my diagnosis as I saw it. However, since you're all right, everybody's happy — And you'll be wanting something to eat. I'd better tell Aunt.'

'No need. I've already told her: she said she'd bring in sandwiches — '

Bob nodded and became silent, wondering if Campbell had got out of the house yet. Probably he had. Certainly Aunt Bertha would not have heard anything.

'Bob — ' Eva got to her feet and strolled pensively about the lounge.

'Yes, dear?'

'What was that ambulance doing at the gate when I arrived?' Eva paused at the window and drew back the drapes. 'It's gone now, I notice.'

'Er — yes. A patient arrived in it for treatment. I gave it him and he said he'd see himself out. So presumably he's done so.'

Good! The ambulance had gone, which meant Campbell had made it successfully.

'You mean you actually left a patient to see himself into the ambulance whilst you fixed the furnace fire in the basement?'

Bob got to his feet. 'I believe in letting a patient fight for himself if possible. Builds up confidence. Wasn't anything very much, anyway. Gammy leg.'

'Oh!'

What Eva would probably have said

Bob did not dare to think, but fortunately for him Aunt Bertha came in at that moment, as wooden as ever, bearing a tray full of sandwiches, coffee percolator, and all the etceteras. She set it down on the occasional table.

'If you want anything more just tell me,' she invited, and went out again.

Eva sat down again and busied herself with the coffee. Bob watched her and shifted nervously over and over again. When Eva was silent he was always uncomfortable — but apparently she was no longer thinking of the mysterious patient with the gammy leg, for she resumed conversation with:

'It was lovely in the South of France. Warm and cosy. I could have stayed there for ever.'

'Then why didn't — Why did you come back?'

'Well, I thought you'd be lonely and finding things monotonous. Small practice, dreary waiting, nothing happening — We manage to make it bearable when we're together.'

'Of course, dear,' Bob smiled, though

his eyes were glassy.

Nurse Addison's eyes were glassy too, but mainly with the freezing wind in which she had stood for hours to survey the Cranston home. She had seen everything, and yet nothing, and wasted no time in reporting the fact over the phone to Sir James Barcroft, whom she finally managed to catch at his home.

'I just don't understand it, Sir James!' Nurse Addison declared. 'Twice an ambulance has drawn up — once during the day and once this evening, yet nobody has been brought out of it or put into it. I did see somebody leap out — who obviously was not a patient — and this same person leapt in again this evening. I am at a complete loss.'

'Mmm, all very extraordinary,' Sir James commented, unaware he had made a profound understatement. 'Was the ambulance one of the M.C. fleet or a private one?'

'Definitely a private one. There is, of course, no law against a doctor sending for one — but I cannot understand why nobody was put into it.'

Much throat-clearing at the other end of the wire, then: 'It would seem, Nurse Addison, that Dr. Cranston — and possibly Dr. Campbell too — are engaged on most unprofessional pursuits, and we shall have to take action. For the moment, though, for reasons that I outlined to you earlier, it would be as well if you still kept impersonal watch. You may happen on to something.'

'Quite, quite!'

'Very well then, we will leave it at that — '

'Possibly,' the ex-matron intervened, 'there may be a little more sanity in the proceedings from here on, because Dr. Cranston's wife has returned home. I believe she was in the South of France. I will observe if there is any change of procedure.'

'Capital! And I know we can rely on you, Nurse.'

Nurse Addison smiled wintrily to herself. She was being trusted by the President of the Medical Council! So, quite unaware she was being had for a sucker she put the phone back on its rest and stepped out into the bitter night.

Definitely it was bitter, too — one of the coldest nights of the winter. And therein lay a certain danger for Bob, for some time after he and Eva had finished their sandwiches and coffee and were idling in armchairs in the lounge, Eva suddenly gave a shudder and hugged her shoulders.

'Gosh, but it's cold!' she complained. 'Either the temperature outside has taken a nose-dive or else I feel it more coming from the South of France.'

'Cold?' Bob looked up from the medical treatise that he was reading in order to prevent awkward questions. 'I hadn't noticed. Queer that, because men feel changes of temperature much quicker than a woman. Matter of subcutaneous tissue, you know — '

'The pathological reason doesn't concern me. I think the furnace has gone out. I'd better go and see.'

Eva got to her feet, but Bob literally shot to his. He reached the door before Eva and strove to look casual.

'I'll do it, dear: no job for you. Aunt

must have forgotten all about it. I asked the old dear to keep it going, but maybe she misunderstood.'

'Highly probable.' Eva rubbed the outsides of her arms vigorously. 'Fix it up then before I freeze to death!'

Bob left the lounge with indecent haste and shut the door. In a matter of seconds he had fled into the basement and found the furnace all but out, completely overlooked by the deaf old dear who was at present rolled up in bed with a juicy romantic novel, her domestic activities finished for the day.

Bob worked hard. He put fuel on the fire, blew on it until his head spun, and glanced occasionally at Claire in her tube. No change. She was motionless, glazed, the interior struts of the tube wearing fur coats of frost.

'Is it the furnace, Bob?'

'Eh?' Bob swung frantically, expecting to see Eva descending the basement steps. Apparently she had not decided to do so, however, since only her voice floated from the upper doorway.

'Yes — yes, it's all right now.' Bob

positively chattered. 'Everything will be fine, dear!'

'So I should hope.' Eva turned away from the basement doorway and headed back towards the lounge, then as the phone rang she turned to it.

'That you, Bob? 'The Campbells are Coming' at two o'clock. Right?'

'I suppose so,' Eva answered wonderingly, and listened to something like a gasp at the other end of the wire.

'Bob, is that you?'

'This is Mrs. Cranston speaking. Would you mind repeating that message?'

'Very well. Just tell him 'The Campbells are Coming' at two o'clock. He'll understand.'

'I'm delighted to hear it. Goodbye.'

Eva put the phone down and stood thinking. She was still thinking when Bob reappeared from the basement. Catching sight of her he endeavoured to look unconcerned.

'Be warm enough now, dear. I'll just wash my hands — '

'Bob, just a minute. Somebody has just sent a message.'

'Not a patient?' Bob looked alarmed. The last thing he wanted was to be compelled to leave the house.

'I hardly know. He just said to tell you — 'The Campbell's are Coming' at two o'clock.'

'Are they? I mean, did he? How strange!'

'Very. It wouldn't refer to Dr. Campbell, would it? That doctor who sought your advice just before I went away?'

'Good Lord, no! Probably means two patients — or more — of that name will be here at two tomorrow. That would be a tip-off from the Health Organization, you know. They're very cryptic.'

Eva stared, and before she had a chance to collect her wits Bob fled to wash the dirt from his hands. When he came back into the lounge he looked at her under his eyes and stole to the armchair. He had just raised the medical treatise to continue reading it when Eva spoke.

'You know, Bob, 'The Campbells are Coming' is a traditional Scottish air.'

'I know. Quite a coincidence.'

'If it is a coincidence.' Eva's blue eyes were by now very bright with interrogation. 'Candidly, Bob, I'm a bit puzzled by your manner. Ever since I came home you've been like a cat on hot bricks. Is anything the matter?'

'Nothing more than usual. If I seem to jump about a lot it's because I'm cold. In January I always move about like a Chinaman. You know — short steps, hands in sleeves, body bent — '

'Be serious, can't you!' Eva was becoming indignant. 'I think something is going on! First, Ella vanishes — for some reason that is not at all clear. Second, Aunt Bertha either can't or won't hear me when I ask her point-blank questions. Thirdly, this 'Campbells are Coming' business — '

Bob sighed but he thought fast. 'It simply means, dear, that two people by the name of Campbell — no relation to the Dr. Campbell you're thinking about — will be arriving here at two tomorrow for a diagnosis. I've known about it for a day or two, and the Health Organization said they'd state the time later. Now they have done it.'

'They wouldn't be connected with that ambulance I saw, I suppose?'

'Well — er — Remotely maybe. That was another Campbell, a branch of the same family. They all have gammy legs. A kind of localized arthritis, far as I can discover.'

Eva gazed steadily for a moment or two, then she got to her feet. Bob rose immediately, his face anxious.

'Why such gallantry?' Eva asked dryly. 'I know you used to pop up and down like a jack-in-the-box every time I rose — but that was before we were married. Why do it now?'

'I dunno. Just plain courtesy, I suppose. Er — where are you going?'

'To bed. It's the only place where I'll keep warm. I think we'd better have the heating engineers to look at the furnace: it isn't working at all well. I wish now we'd installed more modern central heating when we bought this old house!'

With which Eva took her departure. Bob watched her go and, slightly opening the lounge door, he also watched her hurry quickly upstairs. Evidently no suspicions concerning the basement had crossed her mind. Quite definitely they had not, but since she was not entirely a fool she was determined to sleep with one eye open and see if anything came of 'The Campbells are Coming.' She had not, as Bob had hoped, overlooked the fact that there are two two o'clocks in twenty-four hours.

Bob, left to himself, sat with brow wrinkled as he tried to figure out what to do next. Clearly, Campbell would come at two a.m., and somehow Claire would have to be smuggled out if at all possible. All this jiggery-pokery was bad enough, but what made it worse was the lack of solution to the real problem — how to awaken the girl.

The front door bell ringing viciously started Bob out of his cogitations. He wondered if Eva had heard it and whether she'd come down to investigate. Eva had heard, but feeling that it might be a legitimate patient she stayed where she was, trying to keep warm and listening intently.

Bob opened the front door and gazed out upon the blue nose and magnificent bosom of Nurse Addison. He was not sure which looked the coldest — her eyes or the frost on die pathway.

'Good evening, doctor! You'll forgive the lateness!'

It was not a question, but a statement; then the ex-matron was in the hall, her breath hanging like dragon's smoke.

'You are certainly diligent, Nurse,' Bob commented, shutting the door. 'Go into the lounge, please — '

He followed her in, remarking to himself that Eva had been right. The air inside was not much warmer than outside. The damned central heater must be choked up somewhere.

'Doctor — ' Nurse Addison sat down, square and formidable. 'Doctor, you will be the first to concur, I think, that you and Dr. Campbell engaged me for the specific duty of nurse during the Claire Baxter experiment?'

'I agree. Would you care for a drink?'

'Thank you, no. That being so, and since I am a stickler for duty, I must ask you to let me see the patient. It is quite impossible for me to be kept hanging about in this fashion without knowing how or when the experiment is to finish.'

'I said I would send for you when the dossier was completed.'

'I am aware of it, but I also have the lawful right to tend the patient meanwhile. Who is feeding her? You?'

'Er — no. In her present state she doesn't require any food.'

'That is ridiculous, and you know it! No matter how low her pulse or thread of life she needs nourishment. I insist that I give it to her.'

'I'd remind you, Nurse, that I am the doctor. You will do as I say.'

'In normal circumstances I would be delighted to co-operate, but the present circumstances are baffling in the extreme. Unless I am at least allowed to see the patient I shall feel compelled to report your peculiar evasiveness to the Medical Council.'

'Oh — ' Bob muttered something under his breath. 'Very well, since you are so zealous, Nurse. Please come into the basement.'

Nurse Addison rose. 'Might I enquire why you no longer use the surgery?'

'Claire is undergoing special external heat treatment. The furnace is the best means of producing it. Come.'

Bob opened the door and at length the ex-matron found herself in the cobwebby basement, the furnace on one side and a stacked pile of fuel on the other. Her face smudged and suspicious she gazed at the delectable, immovable Claire. Then her merciless eyes moved back to Bob.

'I believe you said you did revive her and then reduced her to a coma again?'

'To study her reactions for my dossier, yes.'

Long silence. Bob perspired gently and kept his ear cocked. With every second that passed he was expecting to hear the feet of Eva descending the stairs into the basement, but nothing happened. And it was during this insufferable calm that Nurse Addison pinpointed her gimlet eyes on to Claire, watching her with an unwavering stare.

'I believe,' the ex-matron said finally, 'that this girl is dead!'

'Ridiculous!' Bob retorted. 'You have had enough experience of this case to know that extreme molecular slowness produces a corresponding decrease in the action of heart and lungs. She isn't dead: she just looks that way.'

'None the less I am entitled to my opinion. Might I ask your exact reason for having her near this furnace? Apparently the furnace is nearly out and there is certainly no sign of the frost thawing inside this tube.'

'I do not feel it incumbent on me to explain everything as I go along, Nurse Addison! You'd oblige me by leaving and return when you are sent for!'

The ex-matron compressed her lips. 'Very well, if you wish it that way!'

She turned away angrily and marched up the cellar steps with Bob behind her. Without uttering another word she took her departure, and Bob closed the front door sharply and locked it. His earlier belief that Nurse Addison was going to be an infernal nuisance before she was finished was now more than confirmed. The only hope was that she would not take precipitate action: if she held her hand for awhile there might still be a chance of getting Claire out of the house.

In a thoroughly disgruntled mood Bob finally went up to bed. He did not switch on the light for fear of waking Eva. From the sound of things she was dead asleep — but she was not. She was still wondering about 'The Campbells are Coming.'

Just in case Eva might happen to awake, Bob undressed in the normal way and scrambled into his pyjama suit, even though he knew he would probably have to venture outside quite a deal in the bitter air before the night was over.

Meanwhile, Sir James Barcroft, the President of the Medical Association, was stirring uneasily as the extension telephone rang beside his bed. Shaking the sleep out of his head he dragged the instrument to him.

'Yes? Barcroft speaking — '

'Nurse Addison speaking, Sir James — '

'Great heavens, Nurse, don't you ever

go to bed? It's not far from one o'clock.'

'I am aware of it, sir, but I couldn't rest until I reported my experiences this evening. I paid a late call on Dr. Cranston — a surprise call indeed — and I was gravely disturbed both by his manner towards me and what I saw —'

'Indeed?' Sir James yawned and closed his eyes. 'And what did you see?'

Nurse Addison's voice lowered. 'I saw Claire Baxter, the unhappy victim of Dr. Cranston's appalling experiment. I beheld her as she was on the occasion of the first test — almost naked and covered in frost, lying within a sealed tube. I do not suggest for a moment that there is anything immoral in Dr. Cranston's experiments — aided and abetted by Dr. Campbell — but I do feel with everything that is in me that that girl is dead!'

Sir James shot upright. 'Dead! Dead, did you say?'

'That is what I think. There is also another grimly significant factor: Dr. Cranston has moved the body into the furnace basement. He gave me a very unconvincing explanation about trying to thaw her out, but I saw no trace of such a phenomenon. I am left wondering if perhaps he was intending — '

'Good Lord! Not burn the body!'

'I don't know. That would be a dangerous statement, but I am entitled to think what I like, and so are you.'

By this time the President was fully awake. He frowned in thought for a moment, then:

'It would appear that things are getting out of hand, Nurse, and you are to be congratulated upon your diligence. I had hoped that Doctors Cranston and Campbell would be able to explain everything and thereby benefit medical science, but if — as seems likely — their experiment has gone wrong and they are trying to hide a corpse we must take immediate action. Leave everything to me. I'll deal with it.'

'Quite, quite! I am more than relieved, Sir James.'

The President rang off, and at the other end of the wire Nurse Addison stood smiling complacently, a formidable figure in dressing gown and cap.

'I fancy, Dr. Cranston, that you will not again try and baulk me in the course of my duty,' she muttered, and thoroughly satisfied she had done everything necessary she prepared for a belated retirement to bed. And Bob remained awake, counting the minutes, thinking deeply, more or less certain that Eva was fast asleep even though her heavier breathing had now ceased.

'A strong electrical surge to commence with,' Bob muttered. 'A very weak one for the hoped for revival, and yet nothing happened. Wonder why? Damned queer.'

Eva strained her ears, but could not catch the words. She heard the clock on the landing strike half past one, then she stirred and gave an involuntary shiver. Immediately Bob's voice came out of the gloom.

'Anything wrong, dear? Sorry if I disturbed you, but I've only just come to bed.'

Eva could have called him a liar, but she didn't. Instead she sat up and switched on the bedlight. Bob studied her anxiously as she cupped her hands about

122

her plump bare shoulders.

'This house is just like a tomb!' she declared. 'I'm that cold I could scream.'

'You should wear thicker nightclothes after the South of France.'

'You mean the house ought to be properly warm!' Eva retorted. 'Look at that window!'

Bob screwed an eye round and looked. The glass panes were glazed over with fronds of frost.

'We've never had the windows that thick over before,' Eva complained, tugging the bedclothes up to her neck. 'You'd have kept some of the cold out if you'd drawn the curtains. Why didn't you?'

'I thought they'd rasp and disturb you.'

Eva did not say anything, and Bob hoped desperately that she would try to sleep again, particularly as it was heading towards two o'clock. Instead, however, Eva kept the light on and lay peering over the top of the small mountain of bedclothes. Then apparently coming to a sudden decision she scrambled out of bed and pushed her feet into slippers.

'Now what?' Bob demanded. 'Hang it all, Eva, can't we have a bit of peace?'

'Peace? In this mausoleum?' Her blue eyes glared at him from under tumbled blonde hair. 'I'm going to fix that central heating furnace if it takes me the rest of the night!'

She whisked on her gown and drew the girdle tight. By the time she had done so Bob was out of bed and at the door. Very taut but determined he barred the way, dragging on his gown.

'Fixing the furnace is no job for you if you're so cold,' he said flatly. 'You'll probably catch pneumonia or something. I'll do all the fixing.'

'So you said last time, and a grand mess you seem to have made of it! I'll do it this time — and you needn't worry about my catching cold. I'm warm enough in this gown. And tomorrow,' Eva added firmly, 'or rather today, we'll get Ella back whether her father's ill or not. With all due respect to Aunt Bertha she's no use in the place at all — certainly not for keeping the furnace going.'

'I agree,' Bob said promptly. 'You go

back to bed and snuggle down whilst I — '

'Nothing doing, Bob. You're a doctor, not a furnace-man.'

Bob gave it up. He had done all he could, but just the same he did not see remaining here and waiting for the storm to break, so as Eva pulled the door open he quickly fell into step beside her. She gave him an enquiring glance as she switched on the landing light.

'Might as well do it together,' Bob explained. 'And I am sure I ought to do it instead of you — Or better still, let's dig out Aunt Bertha and make it her job. It is really, you know.'

'At her age? Shame on you!'

Plainly there was nothing more could be done, so Bob kept close behind Eva as she hurried down into the furnace basement. As he had expected she slowed up gradually in her descent of the basement steps as she caught sight of the long, transparent tube in its cradle. Because of the haze of cold condensed on the inner side of the tube she could not, from her standpoint, see Claire as yet.

'What's that thing doing there?' Eva glanced up over her shoulder. 'It ought to be in the surgery, oughtn't it?'

'Not exactly, dear. There's a medical reason for it being here.'

'There is? It's going to be difficult to get to the furnace.' Quite unshaken Eva continued her downward course and finally reached the basement floor. She turned immediately to the furnace and unlatched the steel door. Within were almost extinct embers.

'You forgot to stoke up,' she said curtly, and Bob nodded miserably, striving to block the view of the tube by putting himself between it and Eva.

'Well, don't stand there!' Eva continued. 'You don't expect me to haul the fuel about, do you?'

'Eh? Oh no, of course not — ' Bob was compelled to move, and he began to fill the bucket noisily. In the midst of it he heard Eva give a strangled gasp of horror. Then he shut his eyes.

'Bob! Bob! Who on earth is this?'

'Eh?' Bob imagined he sounded casual as he turned. 'Who, dear?'

'Here! Here in this case! This — this woman!'

Bob put some fuel into the furnace whilst he considered what came next. Eva waited stonily until at last he was compelled to meet her coldly accusing eyes.

'Oh, you mean Claire?' Bob laughed lightly. 'Just a volunteer for a medical experiment, dear.'

'I take it you mean *the* experiment, that tomfool theory of yours about freezing people until they're hard as mutton? From the vague hints you've given at times I imagined you had a man for your subject.'

'The man couldn't come. He strained himself, and his sister came instead. This is she — Claire Baxter.'

'Oh — ' Eva looked fixedly into the case, then a horrified expression crossed her face. Bob waited, on the edge of panic.

'All perfectly logical, dear — '

'Perhaps! What on earth is she doing hidden down here instead of being in the surgery? Why did you get rid of Ella? And why did you get rid of me on false pretext?'

'I didn't — '

'Oh yes you did! There was nothing the matter with me: the specialist said so! Now I come home and find this half-dressed hussy in the cellar! If everything's above board why didn't you mention her to me?'

'Because I know how much you despise my scientific experiments — '

Eva swung, too furious to listen any further. Bob watched her flee up the basement steps, and muttered something to himself. He piled more fuel on the reluctant furnace and then sped after her, catching up at last in the bedroom. She was pacing back and forth stormily, her elbows clasped in her crossed hands.

'Don't talk to me!' she flamed as Bob came in. 'The whole thing is horribly clear to me now. No wonder you didn't want me to fix the furnace! No wonder you let the heat die down rather than go into the basement and perhaps have me follow you! I can see now why Aunt Bertha didn't fix the furnace: you didn't dare let her see what you've got down there!'

'Nothing of the kind! She knows all about it!'

'She does, eh?' Eva's eyes glittered. 'We'll soon see!'

She strode from the room, leaving Bob wondering helplessly what was going to happen next. In a moment or two she had returned with the dozy, mob-capped, be-gowned Aunt Bertha beside her.

'Aunt, something serious has happened,' Eva explained. 'There is a woman in the cellar, a woman in a tube. What do you know about her?'

'Nothing,' Aunt Bertha answered stolidly. 'Why wake me up in the middle of the night to ask fool questions?'

Bob moved urgently. 'Listen, Aunt, I know I asked you to keep quiet, but now I want you to speak. Tell Eva everything.'

'I don't know what you're talking about,' Aunt replied impatiently. 'And if you don't mind I'll go back to bed.'

Whether anybody minded or not made no difference, for she departed anyway. Eva turned slowly, hands on her hips.

'So Aunt knows all about it, does she? Bob, I can't begin to tell you how I feel about this! Consider what — '

Eva broke off, frowning. Outside the window on the biting winter air had come a whistled refrain. There was no denying what it was supposed to be — 'The Campbells are Coming, they are, they are! The Campbells are Coming, Hurrah, Hurrah!'

Bob glanced sharply at the electric clock on the dressing table. It was exactly two. Then Eva brushed past him and peered through the frosty glass.

'Who's doing that whistling?' she snapped. 'And don't think it hasn't dawned on me that it's something to do with that idiotic phone call.'

'Probably somebody serenading Aunt,' Bob said sourly.

'At two in the morning, at her age, and deaf as a post?'

'I've had enough of this!' Bob snapped, and he hurried from the bedroom and down the stairs to the front door.

The tall figure of Campbell was on the front step, his overcoat collar up round his ears.

'Well, everything okay?' he asked

genially, stepping into the hall. 'I've got the ambulance out there and — '

'There's no need for it,' Bob muttered. 'Eva has discovered the whole thing and blown the roof sky high. There'd be no point in moving Claire now.'

Campbell thumped his forehead gently. 'Y'know something? This ambulance blighter is going to become stark crazy if I tell him he isn't needed after all! He's staying exclusively on this job because I've paid him well. Can't let the M.C. know what we're up to, you know.'

Bob sighed. 'We hardly need to. I think Nurse Addison will do that for us.'

Campbell seemed about to reply, then he looked beyond Bob and smiled genially.

'Good evening, Mrs. Cranston — or rather morning.'

Bob turned. Eva had come silently down the stairs, as pretty as a picture with her hair loosened. With her thumbs latched in the girdle of her gown she looked from her husband to Campbell, then back to Bob again.

'I'm sorry, Bob,' she said quietly. 'I

131

shouldn't have flown off the handle like that. Crazy you may be in regard to medical experiments, but I know you're morally sound.'

'How very interesting.'

Campbell grinned, and Eva looked at him crossly. 'Up to now I've only heard about you, Dr. Campbell, and never met you.'

'Then shake hands,' Bob said, smiling in relief. 'My wife — Dr. Campbell.'

'Matter of fact,' Eva continued as the powerful fingers left hers, 'I blame you for most of the mess which poor Bob seems to be in. I seem to recall that you were the one who thought of a volunteer for his fantastic suspended animation experiment?'

'Correct, Mrs. Cranston. And it isn't fantastic — We have, however, run into one or two snags.'

'I've noticed that.'

'Not in that sense, I don't mean. The trouble is that having put Claire into suspended animation we can't wake her up again. Tried everything we can think of.'

'Which is why she's in the basement,' Bob put in triumphantly. 'I got the idea, apparently a wrong one, that she might thaw out near the furnace.'

Eva frowned. 'Sure she isn't dead, and just preserved by the cold?'

'Certain!' Bob hesitated and gave Campbell a startled look. 'At least I think I am! We haven't made a check on her reactions since she was taken into the basement. Come to think of it, Nurse Addison swore she was dead too.'

'Wish I'd never called that woman in,' Campbell growled. 'I only did for the ethical side of the thing — Better check up on Claire, Bob. This may be more serious than it looks. How about the instruments? Where are they?'

'Still in the surgery. I disconnected them from the tube when we took it below — Aunt Bertha and myself, I mean.'

'Well do we take the instruments down to the tube, or bring the tube back to the instruments?'

'I prefer leaving her where she is. I still think that heat may finally achieve something.' Bob glanced at Eva. 'Thanks for being understanding, dear. We're in trouble enough as it is. You'd better go back to bed.'

'Not a bit; I'm too interested. I'll help.'

5

Arrested for Murder

So during the next hour the instruments essential to testing Claire's reactions within the tube were transported to the basement. Campbell only took time out to dismiss the sulphuric ambulance man, then he returned into the house to help Bob and Eva. It was nearly half past three when the final connections had been made.

'All this is quite intriguing,' Eva commented, surveying the apparatus. 'If you'd taken me into your confidence before this, Bob, I'd probably have been a lot more co-operative.'

Bob smiled whimsically. 'This is a fine time to think of it! Anyway, we'd better get to work. Just stand and watch, Eva: you'll see for yourself that Claire is still alive no matter how dead she looks to the eye. Ready, Boris?'

135

'More than.' Campbell took up his position before the big heartbeat register. Bob moved across to the small generator, which was used only for reaction purposes, as distinct from the bigger generator that had powered the original frequencies.

'Just the same,' Campbell said after a moment, obviously relieved. 'Sixteen beats to the minute.'

'Temperature minus one twenty,' Bob added. 'That makes things just as they were before. Apparently the furnace hasn't helped any. Not that I really thought it would, since the tube insulates temperature outside as much as it does inside.'

'Did you say sixteen beats to the minute?' Eva asked as Bob switched off. 'How on earth does she stay alive at that slow pulse rate? It ought to be — er — seventy-two, oughtn't it?'

'Normally, yes. She stays alive because every other part of her body has slowed down in step, therefore no undue strain is placed on any particular organ or set of nerves. Fact remains that she isn't dead, and that is all that signifies.'

'Except the trifling matter of reviving her,' Campbell said, gloomily for him.

Eva pondered for a moment. Then: 'Surely it's a case of what goes up must come down?'

The two men looked at her. She gestured.

'I don't know anything about science or medicine, but it seems logical to me that if you reduced her to zero, or whatever it is, you should be able to restore her by an exact reversal of the process.'

Bob smiled sadly. 'It isn't as easy as that, Eva. A time-factor enters into it. It is quite on the cards that ten years may have to elapse before she comes round.'

'Ten years! But how in the world do you propose to explain things? The authorities will be after you long before then.'

'Have to tackle that when it comes, that's all. We've tried everything we can think of, without result.'

'Down here, do you mean, or in the surgery?'

'In the surgery: the main equipment is

up there. No use trying again here. The answer would be just the same. Matter of fact,' Bob sighed, 'I haven't a single clue in the whole thing. And yet, back of my mind, I keep pondering the fact that we used electrical energy some eight or ten times more powerful for the original freeze than we did for the attempted restoration. I feel, vaguely, that the mistake lies somewhere there — '

'And meantime she just lies there?' Eva looked at Claire in the frosty depths of the tube.

'Unhappily, yes,' Campbell replied. 'Nothing else we can do until a bright solution strikes us. My only fear is that the answer may not be found for many, many years, during which time I'll become an old man, so old that Claire will probably laugh her head off if I ask her to marry me. That's a point, you know,' he added, looking at Bob. 'She's ageless — timeless — whereas we are advancing in the usual way.'

Bob said nothing. Eva drifted towards the closed door of the furnace and basked in the heat radiating from it. At last

Campbell stirred himself and glanced at his watch.

'Well, I may as well get back home. Might grab a bit of sleep before the cares of the day start again. I don't see what more we can do, Bob, until we can think of some new line of restoration.'

'I'll never stop thinking it over,' Bob promised, and led the way up the steps to see Campbell off the premises. When he turned from closing the front door he beheld Eva waiting for him to return to bed.

'Say, is she brittle?' she asked, looking rather startled.

'Claire? I imagine so.'

'Then won't you have to be particularly careful when you start moving her about in that tube? Suppose she got a jolt? Her legs, or head, or something might drop off!'

Bob shuddered. 'Don't be so ghoulish, woman! Anyway I don't think that would happen. This isn't ordinary freezing whereby the body sets hard as iron: it's an all-over slowing down of molecular warmth, which automatically means she radiates less molecular warmth than normally. I don't think she'd break as would an ordinary petrified object.'

'Let's hope not,' Eva said, commencing to ascend the stairs. 'And there's something else, Bob — I can see the value of your discovery now. Bloodless surgery would be possible on a body as immobile and cold as that. But how would the surgeon go to work? He wouldn't be able to touch her, would he?'

'He wouldn't need to. I've got everything worked out for that part of the business. Automatic artificial hands that would work through the tube, guided by radio control, and operated by the surgeon himself. The surgeon using this new technique would be more of a technician than a medical man. An entirely new era in pathology would come in. If only I could bring Claire back to normal!'

Together Bob and Eva had reached the top of the stairs.

'There is an answer!' he told her fiercely.

'If there is, you'll find it.' She smiled at

him rather shyly. 'I'm still sorry I didn't know so much before, otherwise I would not have acted like a ridiculously suspicious wife. I'll try and think of something myself, too. Never know — '

* * *

It was ten o'clock before Bob and Eva awakened the following morning, and then it was only the insistence of Aunt Bertha that got them moving. The night had tired them more than they had realized.

Immediately after breakfast Bob made a routine trip into the basement to be sure things were exactly the same — which they were — then he returned above to try and nail himself down to the ordinary routine of his profession. There were patients to be considered and surgery hours to be held. Eva, he discovered, was in the midst of writing a letter to Ella, telling her to return as soon as practicable.

So to mid-morning. Bob had attended to the few surgery patients who were regulars twice a week, when someone who was plainly not a patient was shown in to him by the wooden-faced Aunt Bertha. The man looked official by reason of his peaked cap and uniform, but he was evidently not from the police.

' 'Morning, doctor.'

Bob nodded and muttered a greeting, wondering what was brewing.

'Is it important?' he asked. 'I'm pretty busy.'

'I realize that and I'll try not to bother you more than I can help. I'm from the Electricity Authority. My men are outside, waiting for you to say the word.'

Bob stared blankly. 'The word about what? What on earth are you talking about, man?'

'We're investigating a matter of overload on our southern line, sir.' The official was very heavy in speech — almost surly. 'Hasn't been in evidence much these last few days, but up to then it happened three times in a week, sometimes by day and sometimes by night. We've had our engineers investigating since then and they've pinpointed the power-line to this spot. Naturally, there are a lot of power-lines, thousands of 'em, but the excess load was always taken up by the one line coming this way.'

'Very interesting, but what in blazes has that got to do with me?'

'That, doctor, I don't know.' Brooding suspicion was in the slightly bloodshot eyes. ' 'Less you've been using a whale of a lot of power and not been aware of it. Can't do that without permission, y'know. Breach of the regulations.'

'This is ridiculous!' Bob protested. 'I've never used any excess at any time. If I had intended to do so I'd have made the proper application.'

'Yes, doctor, I'm sure you would. I'm trying not to say anything out of place, believe me. It does happen sometimes, though, that electrical energy is used without your being aware of it. And that's what we want to investigate.'

'Without my being aware of it? What the devil do you mean? I'm no amateur with electricity, Inspector, but I haven't the remotest idea what you're talking about.'

'It's like this — ' The Inspector sat down and wheezed a trifle. 'In some factories where big electrical equipment is used there's a field of absorption set up — at least that's what it's called. The field drains power from other electrical machines and the power lines feeding them. Technical term is 'dampening', whereby a greater field absorbs a lesser.'

'Elementary,' Bob said, shrugging. 'I know all about that, but what has it to do with my case?'

'I don't know, frankly.' The Inspector stood up again. 'All I do know is that our detectors show the power-line traveling under your house here is the one affected. As it happens, your house is the only one directly over the power-line. Otherwise it travels under fields, streets, and so forth to the power station. Mind if we check your apparatus for unsuspected dampening properties?'

'I've no choice. Carry on; I'm as interested as you are.'

Definitely puzzled, Bob lounged in a far corner, pondering whilst the Inspector departed. He soon returned with two engineers, both of them loaded with all manner of electrical gadgets. In silence Bob watched them go to work. They tested everything within sight, including the infrared and ultra-violet lamps. Finally they came to the disconnected generator, which had supplied power for Claire's descent into sub-zero.

'Use this generator much?' the Inspector questioned, and Bob shrugged.

'Very little. It's part of a special experiment.'

The Inspector nodded and motioned his men to continue their investigation. The generator was started up and instruments passed around it and examined. Finally the whining ceased and the engineers shrugged negatively.

'Entirely normal,' one of them said, and the Inspector looked puzzled.

'Fault may be below ground then,' he decided. 'Certainly it doesn't seem to be here. All right, boys — that's it.'

The engineers departed and Bob raised an enquiring eyebrow as the Inspector stood thinking.

'Are you satisfied with just this

surgery?' he asked. 'Don't you want to examine the whole house?'

Bob realized that if the answer to this one was 'Yes' he would have to move fast to somehow get Claire and her tube out of sight. But to his relief the Inspector shook his head.

'Won't be necessary, sir. The bulk of your electrical stuff is in this surgery: the rest won't amount to anything. According to the records you have a refrigerator, television, radio, electric iron, electric cooker, vacuum, and ordinary electric light fittings. None of those could be responsible. You have no electric fires because of solid fuel central heating.'

'Right,' Bob acknowledged, breathing again.

'Mmm — then there's nothing more wanted here. In any case the power-line we're bothered about passes directly under this part of your house, and no other part — so any other part of the house wouldn't enter into it.'

'I see. Just how deep is this power-line?'

'Oh, around five feet down. High voltage. Anyway, sorry to have troubled you this way. Thanks for the co-operation.'

Bob nodded and with that the Inspector went on his way. The front door had barely closed upon him before Eva came hurrying in. She was looking anxious.

'What on earth did he want with those men and instruments? Anything to do with Claire? In case they went into the basement I threw a dust sheet over Claire's case.'

'Good girl! Matter of fact they're from the Electricity Authority, investigating an overload on their southern line — ' and Bob gave the details.

'Then what's the answer?' Eva asked, puzzled.

'Lord knows! Since this is the only house situated right over their precious line they suspect me of pinching current to which I'm not entitled, I suppose — '

Bob paused and looked up rather wearily as Aunt Bertha appeared in the surgery doorway.

'An Inspector to see you, boy.'

'What, again? He's only just left — '

'Different one this time,' Aunt Bertha said phlegmatically. 'Police, I think.'

Bob's expression changed and Eva caught at his arm. 'I can see them, if you like. Give you a chance to think things out.'

'Never mind. I'll tackle it — Ask him in, Aunt, please.'

Aunt Bertha shrugged and returned into the hall. After a moment three men came into the surgery — not one. They were quietly-dressed, broad-shouldered, with a certain 'something' about them.

'Dr. Cranston?' the tallest, middle-aged one enquired, pleasantly enough.

'The same — ' and Bob found himself looking at a warrant card.

'I'm a police inspector, doctor. I'd like a word with you privately, if you don't mind.'

'Certainly.' Bob felt rather sick and gave Eva a glance of dismissal. When she had gone the police inspector unbent a trifle. 'These gentlemen are Detective-Sergeant Wallis and Dr. Blair, of our pathological department.'

Bob inclined his head and waited, standing the scrutiny of the Inspector's calm gray eyes.

'I am here, Dr. Cranston, at the request of the President of the Medical Council. It appears he is somewhat disturbed by certain facts which have come into his possession. Concerning a young woman by the name of Claire Baxter.'

Bob waited. The Inspector still studied him and then smiled disarmingly.

'Obviously, Dr. Cranston, you are a reputable member of the medical profession, and you must not in any way misconstrue the purpose of this visit — '

'That is somewhat difficult, Inspector, when you bring a sergeant and police surgeon with you.'

'Just the — shall I say, stock-in-trade? The fact is, doctor, the M.C. is anxious to have your assurance that all is well with this girl Claire Baxter. Apparently you have been proceeding with a scientific experiment in direct opposition to the M.C., hence their decision to enquire. The nurse whom you engaged on the case, and also one Dr. Campbell, will be interrogated later if need be. Whether that need will arise will depend upon your own statement.'

'I consider this an affront,' Bob said deliberately. 'I admit to having proceeded with a scientific experiment against the wishes of the Medical Council, mainly because they turned down a brilliant new surgical system I have devised. I have Claire Baxter in my possession, yes — if I may put it that way — but the experiment is not yet completed.'

'I see. And where is this young woman?'

'In a sealed tube, her molecular reactions slowed down to the limit of safety. She is alive, even though she does not appear to be so to the eye.'

'In that case, Dr. Cranston,' the police surgeon put in, 'you will have no objection to my examining her?'

'I have every objection!' Bob retorted. 'For one thing you cannot examine her because she is in a temperature of minus one hundred and twenty below zero. To open the tube now would instantly kill her. Gradual restoration is the answer, and that I will only perform when I

150

consider it expedient.'

The police surgeon shrugged. 'I respect your wishes, Dr. Cranston. I was not aware of the unusual circumstances. There is surely no reason why I cannot see her, though? In fact, I am afraid I must insist upon it.'

Bob hesitated. 'I consider this all very arbitrary, but I suppose I have no choice. Very well, you shall see her. Come this way, gentlemen.'

He led the way to the surgery door and noticed that Eva was in the hall beside the telephone. As he went past her ahead of the three officials Bob murmured a plea.

'For God's sake get Campbell to come over quickly. This business is getting right out of hand — '

'I have. He's on his way.'

'Good girl!'

Still struggling to look professional, Bob led the way into the furnace basement and the men of the law — in which the police surgeon was presumably included — followed after him. Then they stood looking at the glazed girl within the tube.

'Remarkable,' the police surgeon murmured, plainly fascinated. 'I never saw anything like it!'

'No,' admitted the Chief Inspector, grimness in his voice. 'Neither did I! What's the answer, doctor? Dead or alive?'

'Well, now — ' The police surgeon hesitated, peering closely through the glass. Bob watched him narrowly.

'Frankly,' the Inspector said, 'I consider this to be a perfectly ridiculous situation! We are not allowed to touch or examine this girl in the normal medical way! We are compelled to draw conclusions by just looking at her — and that's absurd!'

'I'd be prepared to stake my reputation that this girl is dead,' the police surgeon said presently, pondering.

'That's pure assumption,' Bob snapped. 'She's alive — but only just, her metabolism reduced to — '

'I notice,' the surgeon interrupted, 'that there are rubber traps in the side of this case, sort of lips. Are they for the purpose of inserting something into the case from the outside?'

'That's correct,' Bob admitted, disconcerted that the 'sleeves' had been detected. 'I put those there in case the need arose to supply nourishment to the girl. It is, of course, quite impossible to insert the naked hand into that temperature, just as we cannot allow external air to reach her. Hence the sleeves.'

The police surgeon gazed in wonder. 'Did you say in case she needed nourishment? Surely she does?'

'No.' Bob shook his head. 'Her life beat is at such a low ebb nourishment is not needed — or if it is, it can only be at extremely long intervals.'

This plunged the surgeon into profound thought, during which the Inspector made an observation after studying his notes.

'I am given to understand, Dr. Cranston, that this girl was revived after the original experiment, and was then returned to this state of suspended animation.'

'The information being supplied by Nurse Addison, I suppose?' Bob asked dryly. 'Yes, it's more or less correct.'

'How 'more or less?' Can you not be more precise?'

As Bob felt around in his mind for an answer the police surgeon spoke again.

'I propose, Dr. Cranston, to make an examination of this girl by means of these sleeve-traps. I can very easily guide the loose end of my stethoscope into the case and test her heart. That long rod over there will do excellently.'

'As you wish,' Bob responded dully, knowing quite well he was in a corner. 'I must warn you, though, not to expect normal reactions from an abnormal subject.'

The police surgeon's response was a grim glance, then he turned to the long thin metal rod in the corner — normally used for drawing across a persistently obstinate window curtain — and busied himself fixing the flexible end of his stethoscope to it, binding it in position with sticking plaster. The job done he carefully inserted stick and stethoscope end into the nearer rubber sleeve and presently stick and stethoscope appeared inside the tube, rapidly coating themselves in hoary frost.

The remainder was sheer manoeuvre as

far as the police surgeon was concerned. By wangling and waving he finally managed to get the end of the stethoscope pressed against the girl's heart and proceeded to listen — and the more he listened the more surprised he looked; then very gradually his face became grim and he looked up sharply.

'As I said earlier, purely from visual observation, this girl is dead.'

'You mean you can't hear her heart?' Bob questioned.

'That is exactly what I mean, and if that isn't proof of death, what is?'

'Normal medical instruments are useless in a case like this,' Bob insisted. 'Of course, you can't hear her heart. It is pulsing at such a low pitch that it is inaudible. But that it is beating at sixteen beats to the minute I can very soon prove to you — '

'Sixteen to the minute! Upon my soul, Dr. Cranston, that is preposterous! Nobody could have a heartbeat that slow.'

'Well, she has!' Bob snapped. 'Until the heart actually stops death cannot be said to have taken place. Now take a look at this — a recording by instruments specially devised for the job.'

It did not take Bob above a few moments to get the heart register into action, and in silence the men watched the ponderous fluctuations of the needle. Sixteen beats to every minute . . .

'Is this possible, doctor?' the Inspector asked sharply, with a glance at the police surgeon.

'By all the laws of medicine and pathology it isn't, but since Dr. Cranston is — '

'Then I refuse to accept it!' the Inspector interrupted. 'According to the stethoscope this girl is dead, and it is upon authorized instruments that all law is built. I have been trained to accept the evidence of my own eyes and I am doing so — To me it appears that this girl is dead, but that her body is being preserved by a freezing process. I'm prepared to swear that anybody else would declare the same thing.'

'And every one of you would be wrong!' Bob retorted. 'What do you suppose that register is for?'

'I don't know,' the Inspector answered, shrugging. 'What I do know is that it is not a piece of apparatus generally accepted by the law and medical profession, therefore I cannot place any faith in it. I shall have to ask you — '

The Inspector broke off and glanced impatiently towards the basement stairs as the lanky figure of Boris Campbell descended them. For once he was looking deadly serious.

'Good morning, gentlemen,' he greeted, arriving at floor level. 'What's this? A delegation?' Then, glancing at Bob: 'Your wife told me you were in some difficulty.'

'Would you be Dr. Campbell?' the Inspector asked curtly.

'I am, yes. What seems to be the trouble?'

'I am placing both you and Dr. Cranston under arrest,' the Chief Inspector retorted. 'You do not have to say anything unless you wish to, but whatever you do say will be taken down and — '

'Never mind the caution,' Campbell interposed. 'What are we being arrested for?'

'The murder of Claire Baxter, whose body we have seen preserved there in that tube.'

'You'd be wiser, Inspector, to investigate this matter to the limit before making dangerous accusations!'

'I have the word of a reputable police surgeon that this young woman is dead and that is enough for me. I must ask both of you to come along with me, gentlemen. Later on I will interview Nurse Addison who also appears to have been mixed up in this business.'

Campbell glanced at Bob. 'What about the heart register? Hasn't the Inspector seen it?'

'He has — but he doesn't believe it. So I'm afraid — ' Bob broke off, his eyes bright. 'Say, wait a minute! You cannot possibly arrest us for murder, Inspector. Claire Baxter wrote an exoneration in case things went wrong. Actually, she is not dead, but since you won't believe it I'll have to make you release us from arrest by reason of her signed statement.'

'I would be interested in seeing it,' the Inspector responded.

Bob stood pondering for a moment, frowning. Then he looked at Campbell.

'That letter Claire wrote — what did we do with it? Hanged if I can remember now.'

The two policemen and surgeon waited in grim calm whilst Campbell pulled at his lower lip and strove to remember.

'In my overall!' Bob exclaimed abruptly, snapping his fingers. 'There it is — '

He hurried across to it hanging on its hook beside the door and quickly felt in the pockets of the suit he was wearing, the same one in which he had been attired on 'the night.'

'Don't seem to have it,' he said finally. 'I just can't remember what I did with it. Things were so hectic at the time that I — '

'Oh, Lord!' Campbell gasped suddenly, staring before him. 'I do believe I know what happened! Do you remember all that figuring you had to do when we were busy on the experiment? There wasn't time for you to go looking for paper. I remember you snatched a sheet out of your pocket and calculated on that — '

'Yes,' Bob whispered. 'I remember now. Then I threw it away into the paper basket, never dreaming what it was. I'd too many other things on my mind.'

He dived for the waste bin and tipped out the contents, searching amidst the debris frantically. After a moment Campbell's voice reached him mournfully.

'I don't think you're going to find it, Bob. Don't you recall Aunt Bertha saying she'd tidied up the surgery? Why, she even had the bin in her hands when she came and told us!'

Bob straightened slowly, his face drawn. He remembered the whole business now — only too clearly. Wheeling, he ran for the basement stairs, but the Inspector's voice halted him.

'Just a moment, doctor, if you don't mind! Where are you going?'

'To check up what happened to the rubbish from that bin! The exoneration letter is amongst it. My Aunt, who has been acting as housekeeper, can probably help.'

'Go and fetch her, Farrish,' the Inspector ordered the detective-sergeant, so Bob came back slowly into the basement and bit his lower lip worriedly.

'I don't know what day the dustmen call,' he muttered. 'If they've been — '

He looked at Campbell, and all Campbell could do was spread his hands and shrug negatively. Then Aunt Bertha became visible at the top of the steps, grumbling to herself as she came below.

'Taking me away from the cooking,' she complained. 'What is wrong down here, Bobby? The furnace not working?'

'Nothing to do with the furnace, Aunt; something much more important.' He gripped her plump arms tightly. 'Now listen to me carefully. You remember cleaning up this surgery on the night we began the experiment?'

'Merriment?' Aunt Bertha repeated. 'What cause is there for that?'

'Experiment!' Bob screamed. 'The night of the experiment! You cleaned up and emptied the waste bin! Where did you empty it?'

'Dustbin, of course — Most of the stuff was paper.'

Bob wheeled. 'Quickly, Inspector, I

want permission to look at the dustbin or else get the wife to do it.'

'Why?' Aunt Bertha asked stolidly. 'It was emptied yesterday afternoon. I saw the men come.'

Bob stared at her fixedly and swallowed something.

'That does it!' Campbell said, with a whistle. 'Gone up in smoke by now, I suppose, along with tons of other paper — No, there's one chance!' he broke off. 'Some authorities use paper waste for re-pulping. There's a dim chance your particular bit of paper rubbish may be in a certain pile.'

'Get in touch with the cleansing authorities,' the Inspector suggested. 'I'm willing to give you every chance to put this ugly business right. You won't mind the sergeant accompanying you to the 'phone?'

'No choice, have I?' Bob snapped. 'I may as well tell you I strongly resent being treated like a common criminal — All right, Aunt,' he added, 'thanks for coming down here: there's nothing more you can do.'

Aunt Bertha sniffed and turned back to the basement stairs. Bob followed her up, the sergeant behind him. In a few moments the sergeant was standing implacably waiting as Bob dialed the cleansing authority's number. His conversation thereafter was long and difficult. It was even possible the man at the other end thought he was crazy. The final upshot was that his particular load of rubbish, which included all other household waste as well as paper, had long since been consigned to the incinerator.

'Thanks,' Bob muttered, and rang off.

'No luck, doctor?' the sergeant asked, not unsympathetically.

'None. Hell! What a fool I must have been — '

Dismally he returned to the basement and the Inspector listened in grim silence as he was given the details.

'In that case, doctor, I'll have to ask you to come along,' he said. 'You'll be formally charged along with Dr. Campbell, at the station.'

'I never heard of anything so preposterous!' Campbell burst out. 'Will you not see reason, Inspector? This girl is not dead! I'm a doctor and so is Cranston here. Do you suppose we don't know what we're talking about?'

'I am compelled,' the Inspector replied evasively, 'to rely on the opinion of the police surgeon here, and he is quite convinced we are not looking upon a woman with her life slowed up, but one who is dead and refrigerated.'

'And what happens to her now we're arrested?' Bob questioned.

'I'll have to ask the Medical Council about that. For the moment she can stay where she is — '

'Then let me warn you of one thing. If that case is opened the girl really will die! It would mean that, finding her dead, you'd consider your case absolutely complete. Promise me one thing, Inspector — do not open that case under any circumstances whatever.'

'I have no power to promise that, doctor, but I'll see what I can do. Now, we must be getting along — '

6

Eva Intervenes

For Eva, the shock of her husband and Campbell's arrest was a violent one, nor could she think how to act in the dilemma. For a couple of hours after the police, Bob and Campbell had left her home she wandered moodily about the house, trying to get things into proper focus. The one thing predominating her mind now was the fact that Bob had said, over and over again, that Claire was not really dead. The one difficulty was to find the way to revive her.

'And what can I do about that?' Eva asked herself hopelessly. 'I don't even know the nature of the experiment, and if I tamper with anything I might really kill the girl off completely. Oh, if only I knew something of scientific matters!'

There came a diversion for her during the afternoon when the Chief Inspector returned, this time with the pompous Sir James Barcroft, President of the Medical Council.

'What now?' Eva asked both of them bitterly. 'Are you not satisfied with having arrested my husband? Must you turn the house into a rendezvous?'

'I can assure you, madam, nobody regrets this distressing business more than I,' Sir James responded gently. 'I can only ask that you try and understand my viewpoint. I have to act for the Council as a whole, and not necessarily of my own volition.'

'Meaning what?' Eva glanced at him impatiently.

'Meaning that I, personally, have a good deal of faith in your husband's theory of suspended animation.'

'You have? Yet you hound him like this before he has the chance to finish the experiment properly! What kind of a man do you call yourself? How much use are you to the advancement of medicine?'

'Really, madam, I — '

'But for you,' Eva continued bitterly, 'my husband and Dr. Campbell would have been left to finish the great work they have started. As it is there's a ridiculous charge of murder, just because no medical men have instruments cleverly designed enough to show that Claire Baxter still lives!'

The President looked uncomfortable. To the Inspector there was something serio-comic about the way petite Eva confronted the fleshy, prosperous head of the medical profession.

'What,' Eva asked deliberately, her jaw set, 'do you want here now? To hound me?'

'No madam. I am here to look at this body in the tube and decide whether or not the law should remove it for burial. The Inspector here has informed me that your husband insisted the body should not be touched. So I have a grave decision to make.'

'My husband knows more about it than you do,' Eva snapped. 'I've gathered enough myself to know that if you let air into that case, or in any wise alter the temperature, Claire Baxter will really die. Let her be, can't you!'

The President jerked his head. 'Come Inspector, we'd better take a look.'

Eva, her fists clenched at her sides, watched them go. They were absent nearly half an hour, and she wondered in a kind of frustrated horror what they were up to. Her spirits rose a little when she beheld the President's genial smile upon his return into the lounge.

'I have decided that due to the exceptional circumstances the body had better remain where it is,' he announced. 'At least until the entire investigation is complete.'

'Complete?' Eva repeated, astonished. 'How much more is there?'

'Quite a deal,' the Inspector put in. 'The inquest will be adjourned until our enquiries are complete. We have Nurse Addison to interrogate yet, and then we have to discuss many details with Miss Baxter's brother, who should have been the subject in the first place.'

'So,' the President finished, 'the body stays where it is. As the head of the M.C. that is my ruling, and it will be abided by. I am none too sure,' he finished slowly, pondering, 'but what your police surgeon isn't completely wrong, Inspector!'

The Inspector started. 'Wrong! You tell me that now, Sir James, when I have all my evidence ranged up?'

'No blame attaches to you, Inspector; you are simply doing your job as you see it — which is correct. But I, trained to anatomy and medicine, noticed many things about that girl, which lead me to believe she really does still live. Did you notice the veins on the insides of her arms?'

'No. I could hardly see her for glaze.'

'I did,' Sir James mused. 'They are taut and strong, which indicates heart action. A corpse does not have taut veins. Veins deflate when the heart's action ceases.'

'Is there a gleam of hope in that statement?' Eva asked anxiously. 'Will you use it in my husband's defense?'

'I will pass the information on to the defending counsel, certainly. I shall take no actual part in the trial, madam, nor make any personal observation. In my position I cannot afford an individual opinion. Rely on it, though, that I will do all I can — Now we must be going. We shall not need to trouble you further, shall we, Inspector?'

'I think not,' the Inspector answered, obviously not at all happy now as to whether he had made the right move or not in arresting Bob and Campbell.

Eva saw them to the door and then again resumed her aimless wandering about the house. Aunt Bertha saw her at intervals but made no comment. The goings-on in the household were by now far beyond the comprehension of this stolid, unimaginative lady. Eva, for her part, finally finished up in the surgery and looked absently about her. This was more or less foreign territory to her, and she had not the least idea why she had wandered in here anyway. Oh, yes! To see if by any chance that letter of exoneration happened to be anywhere about. It might have rolled out of the waste bin into a concealed corner. Miracles can happen . . .

But they didn't this time. After an hour's intensive search in every place she could think of Eva gave it up. Then her eye travelled, quite by chance, to the hefty-looking book nearby upon which a label had been gummed. It said briefly:

DOSSIER RELATIVE TO THE CLAIRE BAXTER SUB-ZERO MOLECULAR RETARDATION.

With a smile at the grandiloquent phrasing Eva opened the dossier and looked at it. Here before her, penned in Bob's typical medical scrawl, were all the details relative to the experiment. At first they did not make sense, but having an average amount of intelligence, Eva slowly began to see what the process was — and the more she read the more interested she became. For the first time she was discovering the real nature of the process her husband had perfected — the process he had explained to the Medical Council. Here were the details that he had not given her because she had insisted his practice came before 'medical dabblings.'

Finally she took the dossier into the lounge, and sprawling herself on the settee, set to work to read the dry details as thoroughly as possible. Here was a chance to discover what had been done, from which it was logical to infer that she might find how to undo. Where her husband and Campbell were steeped in scientific technicalities, and perhaps could not see wood for trees, she as a simple, untrained outsider might be able to put her finger on the answer. A big assumption, perhaps, but at least within the bounds of possibility.

At half-past four Aunt Bertha brought in tea, eating it and reading her romantic novel whilst Eva also read and chewed by turns. She had one thing to be thankful for: Bob had not spared himself in detailing the experiment, probably because writing it out helped him to try and recall every move he had made. It was all there, even to the exact times when he had made his preliminary tests. Apparently he had tested the suspended animation tube twice before the actual experiment — and these two occasions had been by day. The actual experiment itself had been in the evening at 7.45. All three activities — tests and actual thing — had occurred within one week. Everything was duly notated.

Finally Eva put the dossier down and lay back in the cushions to think. Every word that Bob had spoken to her of the experiment gradually drifted through her mind — and one word in particular — 'dampening.'

'Aunt — ' She opened her eyes and looked across to where Aunt Bertha sat reading. 'Aunt, have you any idea what 'dampening' means?'

'Hampering?'

'Dampening!'

'Oh! A young wife like you ought to know that. You do it to clothes when you iron them — '

'So help me,' Eva whispered to herself, struggling from the settee, 'I'll crown this old girl one day!'

She went across to the bookcase and studied the array carefully. In the main, apart from the small fictional offerings, the books were medical, but here and there her husband's propensity for science was typified in such volumes as 'Laws of Conservation of Energy', 'Theory of

173

Ultra-Dynamics', and 'Electrical Laws and Reactions'. Finally Eva decided on the last one and dragged it from its fellows. It was well thumbed, and in the margins were pencil notes. There seemed to be a number of authors represented, the most familiar being Soddy, the famous authority on matter and energy.

Normally, Eva would have shuddered at having to plough through such technical stuff, but in this case she felt the prodding of urgency. Locked up awaiting trial neither her husband nor Campbell were able to help themselves, so it was up to her.

The more she read the more she managed to extract one salient fact from the vast accumulation of technical data — and this one salient fact was that under certain circumstances the greater charge completely absorbs the lesser, producing thereby what is loosely called a 'dampening' circuit. By and large, the whole thing was as clear as mud to Eva, but this one point she did manage to cling to — and with it fixed rigidly in her mind she read again the dossier notes Bob had made concerning the experiment.

'I'm going to bed, Eva.'

'Eh?' Eva looked up absently from the papers and books that surrounded her upon the settee. 'What did you say, Aunt?'

'I said I'm going to bed, and so should you if you want to brace those jaded nerves of yours! Look at the time! It's half-past eleven.'

'Umph,' Eva grunted, thinking hard.

'I've left you some sandwiches in the kitchen and the percolator's on the simmer-point. Better still,' Aunt continued, suddenly resolved, 'I'll bring them in to you, otherwise you'll go on brooding there all night without nourishment. Doesn't do.'

Eva hardly heard her. On a clean sheet of scratch pad she wrote down swiftly: 'Suspended animation tube tested twice before actual experiment. Tested twice by day. Actual experiment was in the evening at 7.45.'

'Here you are,' Aunt Bertha said annoyingly, putting the tray of sandwiches and coffee on the occasional table.

'Promise me you'll have them — and soon.'

'I promise,' Eva agreed solemnly, and Aunt nodded.

'All right. And don't stay up too late. You'll need all your strength in the days ahead now Bob's in such an awful mess — '

Shaking her head to herself Aunt Bertha went out. Eva, always true to her promise, surged up from the sofa and spent a good fifteen minutes brooding, eating and drinking. Finally she made up her mind and went out to the telephone, dialing the number for Scotland Yard. After which she had a considerable task in trying to explain whom she wished to contact. She did not even know the name of the Chief Inspector concerned with Bob's arrest, but from the sergeant-in-charge she did finally discover he was Chief Inspector Carson and that at this hour he was off duty.

'I expected that,' Eva replied, 'but this is too urgent to wait. Where can I contact him?'

'Sorry, madam, I'm not allowed to

hand on that information. What I will do is get in touch with him and ask him to ring you — that is if he considers it necessary.'

'Necessary!' Eva hooted. 'It's a matter of life and death! Very well, thanks, do that. Goodnight.'

She rang off and began to wander restlessly up and down the hall. After perhaps ten minutes the 'phone rang and she whipped it up immediately.

'Carson speaking,' came the recognizable heavy voice. 'I believe you've been trying to contact me, Mrs. Cranston?'

'Definitely I have. I've tumbled on to something of vital importance and I wish to speak to my husband right away. How can that be arranged?'

'I doubt if you'll be able to speak to him yourself since he is in custody. You might manage it through his counsel — '

'I can't wait that long! I have some scientific information to verify, Inspector, which, if it is correct, will not only prove my husband and Dr. Campbell innocent of the charge brought against them, but will also lead the way to Claire Baxter's revival.'

The Inspector seemed to be thinking; then he said: 'Since your husband has not yet actually come to trial I might be able to arrange it with the Assistant Commissioner so that you talk to your husband in my office tomorrow morning. You will not be allowed to talk privately though. The detective-sergeant and myself will be there.'

'That doesn't signify,' Eva replied quickly. 'Just let me talk to Bob, that's all. Do everything you can, I beg of you.'

'You can be assured of that. If there is any way of helping your husband out of his difficulties I am only too willing to co-operate.'

Eva rang off, more settled in her mind. She was pretty sure that the chief inspector would keep his word. There was, however, still another point in her remarkable chain of reasoning that needed verifying. In actual truth it could wait until morning, but Eva knew she would not sleep a wink if she did not try and get some immediate satisfaction — so she rang the local branch of the Electricity Authority.

The man in charge on night duty presently answered.

'Electricity Authority — Emergency Department. Can I help you?'

'Definitely you can,' Eva replied promptly. 'I want to get in touch with an inspector — one particular inspector. He came this morning to this address: Dr. Cranston, The Poplars, North Alderside Road, to investigate an overload. He brought a couple of engineers with him.'

'That'll be in the Special Enquiry Department, madam. Sorry, I can't help you. Ring up Special Enquiry in the morning and ask for Inspector Paulson. He's the man you want.'

'Do you know his first name?' Eva asked quickly.

'Er — Richard. Does it matter?'

'It might. Thanks anyway. Good night!'

Eva rang off and whipped up the telephone directory, thumbing quickly through the pages until she came to 'p'.

'Paul, Paul, Paulson. Mmm — Clarice Paulson; Doctor Eric Paulson — Ah!

Richard Paulson, Inspector, Electricity Authority. Couldn't be simpler — '

Eva dropped the directory, rang the number, then waited. For a long time the ringing tone persisted, then came a gruff and definitely sleepy voice.

'Paulson here. What's the trouble?'

'Sorry to bother you so late, Inspector,' Eva apologized. 'I am Mrs. Cranston. You remember calling here this morning about an overload?'

'Certainly I remember, but that's a matter of business, madam, and not something to be discussed at this hour. You're talking to my private residence, you know.'

'I'm aware of it. The matter is urgent, Inspector, because of — er — legal proceedings against my husband.'

'What matter? Candidly, madam, I haven't the least idea what you're talking about!'

'I'm coming to it,' Eva said patiently. 'My husband, in telling me about your visit, said that you reported three overloads in all. Three. Is that correct?'

'Yes. We recorded three overloads — '

180

'Two by day and one at night, all within one week?'

'That's right,' the Inspector confirmed. 'Just the same, I still fail to see — '

'Very probably, but you'll be given all the details later. Was the week referred to this week?'

'Yes.' The Inspector sounded completely bewildered, as no doubt he was.

'Good!' Eva's eyes were glowing with triumph. 'Now there is something else. Whether you can answer it or not I don't know. Regarding this overload business on one particular line — the southern line I think you said: do you know exactly, in voltage, how much the overload was?'

'Not offhand, I don't.'

'But it would be exactly recorded? They'd have details of it at the power-house concerned?'

'Why certainly. Really, madam, I just can't fathom the reason for this enquiry. We satisfied ourselves that your husband was not responsible, despite the electrical equipment he possesses, so where is the point of — '

'How do I contact the power-house

concerned?' Eva interposed. 'Anybody particular I should speak to?'

Pause. Presumably Inspector Paulson was gathering his strength.

'I think,' he said finally, 'it would be better if *I* got the information you want. I can ring you back in a quarter of an hour if that will suffice? I have your number.'

'That'll do splendidly — and thanks for the co-operation.' Once again Eva put the 'phone down and resumed her restless pacing of the hall. It was not entirely the restlessness of impatience, either. As she moved, she pondered, and back of her mind she felt convinced that she was on the right track. It was the tremendous coincidence of three tests and three overloads which fascinated her, together with the synchronization of the times. There must be a reason for such a happening.

The fifteen minutes were by no means up when the 'phone rang. Instantly Eva snatched up the instrument from the cradle.

'Get it?' she asked anxiously.

'Yes, here's the information you asked

for. The overload in every case, all three times that is, was identical. It amounted to twelve thousand volts in every case, nearly enough to burn out the line had it been prolonged. Fortunately it was not.'

'No variation on any occasion, then?' Eva scribbled quickly on the 'phone pad. 'Twelve thousand each time?'

'That's it. Now do you mind telling me what all this is about?'

'I would if I could, but at the moment I don't know myself. You'll probably see it in the newspapers later on. Thanks for everything, Inspector, and excuse my haste.'

With that Eva rang off. She had far too much on her mind to be bothered giving detailed explanations to the unimaginative inspector. And besides, as she had said, she was not dead sure yet how the position stood.

Thoughtfully she returned to the lounge, pondering the figure of twelve thousand volts. Then gradually it dawned upon her that there was a limit to her scientific capabilities — excellently though she had done so far. She could not make any further moves until she had seen Bob on the morrow. So she switched off the lights and went upstairs to bed.

★ ★ ★

An early 'phone call from Chief Inspector Carson informed Eva that she could talk to Bob in his — Carson's — office at ten o'clock, for no longer than ten minutes. Even this was a special concession, made in the hope that it might help Bob to establish his innocence. Certainly it was enough for Eva, and she arrived at Scotland Yard dead on time.

She found Bob already in the Inspector's office. He looked tired and troubled, which was hardly to be wondered at, but his face lighted as Eva was shown in.

'Eva! This is marvelous even though I don't know what the dickens it's all about. The Inspector here is remarkably evasive.'

'Probably because he doesn't know what I'm driving at,' Eva responded, sitting in the chair the detective-sergeant drew up for her. 'It'll surprise you to know, Bob, that I've turned into a scientist. Sort of, anyway.'

'Oh?' He looked unconvinced. 'You've never shown any leanings that way.'

'I never had such urgent necessity before. When you were taken away yesterday I found myself thinking about what you'd said at odd times concerning a 'dampening' effect produced by electricity. I made it my business to look into what it means — '

'It simply means a lesser voltage being absorbed by a greater one. It is not a constant factor but a haphazard one. One of the ungovernable laws of electricity.' Bob frowned. 'I've been doing a good deal of thinking about dampening, too, but I don't seem to have got any nearer.'

'That may be because you're right on top of the problem. I'm sort of outside it and therefore can view it more clearly. I also found the dossier on Claire Baxter and read it from end to end. The point that tied up in my mind was that the times you had made tests, as well as the experiment, tallied with the times of overload at the power station.'

Bob's face had become interested. 'That angle never occurred to me — the coincident times, I mean. After all, it may only be a coincidence at that. I'd forgotten all about that overloading business.'

'I thought you had. Fortunately, I didn't. I rang up the Electricity Inspector and from him I got not only the times — which coincide exactly — but also the amount of the voltage overload on each occasion.'

Bob's eyebrows rose. 'You certainly have been busy! What was the voltage?'

'Twelve thousand volts overload on each occasion.'

Bob sat back in his chair, musing. The Chief Inspector gave the Detective-Sergeant a glance, but neither of them made any comment. This interview did not technically concern them.

'Twelve thousand volts,' Eva repeated deliberately. 'I have a hunch I'm playing, Bob, even though an experienced electrician would probably laugh at me. What I want to know is: what voltage did you use to try and bring Claire back to life?'

'Try and bring?' the Inspector interrupted. 'I understood that she had been restored and then returned to suspended animation.'

'I'm referring to the second occasion,' Eva explained glibly. 'What's the answer, Bob?'

'Twelve thousand,' he answered, giving Eva a surprised look. 'Pretty nearly one hundred and fifty thousand for the first part of the job — reducing Claire to subzero — and twelve thousand to bring her back.'

'That,' Eva smiled, 'is all I wanted to know. You see it means — '

'Great heavens, of course!' Bob snapped his fingers. 'I must have been asleep! The normal power-line of the Electricity Authority is in the region of two hundred thousand volts: that is generally known. That means that when I used a hundred and fifty thousand everything was all right: I had enough load to counter-balance the power-line. But when I used the lesser load — twelve thousand — it was absorbed straight into the power-line passing under the surgery and made no effect at all on Claire!'

'In other words,' Eva said, spreading her hands, 'a dampening circuit was set up in which your 'restoration' frequency was completely soaked up. At least that's what I think. One of those peculiarities of electricity which do happen sometimes.'

'They happen quite a lot!' Bob exclaimed. 'There's an example of it in nearly every gale where overhead power-lines are concerned. Get two lines of differing voltages — one greater than the other — swinging towards each other and you get a dip in lights and power from their feed. This must have been a similar case. That powerline under the surgery picked up the load I was using and automatically the excess registered at the power-station end. The anomaly is that I wasn't taking it: I was giving it!' He reflected for a moment. 'Queer, though, that fact didn't show on the meters. They said I was using twelve thousand volts, so how was I to know any differently?'

'The soaking up process must have come between the transmission of the power from your generator and the tube in which Claire was lying,' Eva said thoughtfully. 'The power passed the meters all right and registered itself, but it didn't get to its 'destination'. Possibly those floor cables were not insulated enough to do the trick.'

'By everything, that's queer,' Bob breathed. 'I do believe you've stumbled on the answer, Eva!' He turned urgently to the Inspector. 'Inspector, I've got to be released! I must make a different test with that tube and prove my point — and my innocence. You've heard this conversation: surely you see the possibilities?'

'Certainly I do, and from the sound of things your wife — for an amateur — has done a pretty good piece of reasoning. Unfortunately, Doctor, I am bound by the law and I cannot release you. I am not allowed to take cognizance of theories.'

'But damnit, man, this isn't just a theory! It's the right answer. I've just got to be allowed to prove it.'

The Chief Inspector shook his head. 'Sorry. Can't be done.'

'In that case,' Eva said, 'I must try for myself. Can you trust me sufficiently, Bob, to try my idea out?'

'Depends what you propose doing.'

'Revive Claire, of course!'

'Since you have done it once,' the Inspector said slowly, 'why all this difficulty and theorizing over doing it again? Or have you never revived her? You might as well be frank about it, doctor.'

Bob sighed. 'All right — I've never revived her. That can now be testified. She is not dead, though, no matter what your police surgeon says.'

'Time's up,' the Detective-Sergeant announced impassively, at which Eva got to her feet.

'You'll have to rely on me to finish the job, Bob — and having got this far I'm pretty sure I will. Don't get down-hearted.'

He smiled rather wanly, then as the Inspector spoke Eva turned to him.

'The formal charge before the magistrates will be this morning,' he said. 'Your husband, Dr. Campbell, and Nurse Addison will all be indicted, and I expect committed for trial. The trial cannot take place before another week at least, so if you have something definite to offer within that time let me know immediately and I'll take the necessary steps.'

'Thanks, I will.' Eva shook hands and gave a grateful smile, then after a kiss on Bob's rather drooping mouth she left the office and headed straight for home. She arrived to find Aunt Bertha on the point of leaving and Ella back on duty.

'It's a bad thing about Bob,' Aunt Bertha said, shaking her head. 'Shouldn't dabble in things he doesn't understand. I'm sorry for you, my dear — mighty sorry.'

'You don't have to be,' Eva replied brightly. 'This is most probably the darkest hour before the dawn. Anyway, thanks for everything you've done to help, and you do see there's no point in staying on now Ella's back?'

Aunt Bertha gave her stolid smile and said no more. She went down to the waiting taxi at the kerb and Eva went quickly into the house. Ella was in the midst of tidying the lounge.

'It's a dreadful thing about the master, m'm!' she exclaimed. 'I don't rightly understand what happened, an' even less why he sent me away for a holiday. Matter of fact I'm glad to be back. I've nothing to do at home.'

'No, I'm sure you haven't,' Eva agreed absently.

'Begging your pardon, m'm, but what am I to do about the young lady down in the furnace cellar? I noticed her when I went to fix the heater. Struck me as sort of pretty, she did, but proper frozen!'

'Frozen is right!' Eva responded. 'You needn't do anything about her, Ella: that's my job exclusively. You just carry on with your normal duties, but don't bother about the furnace. I shall be down there to keep an eye on it.'

'Yes, m'm. Just as you say.'

Eva still pondered, not exactly funking the job that lay below in the basement, but nonetheless conscious of the great responsibility that rested upon her. Finally she made up her mind, went to the surgery for Bob's dossier, and then made her way below.

Reaching the tube she surveyed it speculatively, then took a closer look at the girl inside. The task now was to follow out exactly the restoration process as given in the dossier, and as far as Eva could see there was no reason why it should not work correctly. Here, in the basement, the absorptive power of the southern cable ought not to be operative since it only passed under the surgery, and that was situated some little distance away — far enough, anyhow, Eva reasoned, to be innocuous.

Moving to the switch panel she examined it carefully, and after a while it dawned upon her that only the 'registration' instruments were located here. She remembered having helped to bring them down. The main apparatus, the bulky stuff concerned with the experiment itself, were bedded down in the surgery, including the main generator.

'Oh, gosh!' Eva whispered, dismayed. 'Now what do I do? I can't work in the surgery because that's where the trouble is. On the other hand, even if it were possible to transfer all the equipment down here I wouldn't know how to link it up.'

Here indeed was a large size in snags,

and not a great deal of time in which to think it out, either. Finally Eva turned back to the dossier and went through it quickly until she came to the complicated circuit diagram referring to every detail of the suspended animation tube. It made her head spin to look at it. Even a television receiver would have seemed simple by comparison. But at least it gave her an insight to her husband's unusual scientific ability. For the first time in her life she found herself admiring this facet of him.

Then back to the immediate problem. Something had to be done. In the end there seemed to be but one answer — go to the fountain head. Which was exactly what Eva did.

Hurrying upstairs again she raced across to the telephone table and quickly searched the directory until she found the number of the Medical Council. In a matter of moments she was through to the organization.

'Sir James Barcroft, please,' she requested, as a singsong voice greeted her. 'Extremely urgent.'

'I'll just see if Sir James is present, madam. The name please?'

'Mrs. Doctor Robert Cranston.'

'Hold the line — '

Eva not only held the line but her breath as well. She knew it was audacity in excelsis to thus tackle the great man himself, but after all he had said he was inclined to believe in Bob . . .

'Hello, Mrs. Cranston! Barcroft speaking.'

Eva started and then gave a sigh of relief. 'Oh! Thank heaven, Sir James. I was half-afraid I wouldn't catch you. I need your help desperately — and you can also do yourself a good deal of benefit.'

'Really? In what way?'

'Since you are the President of the Medical Council,' Eva hurried on, suddenly resorting to the subtle strategy of her sex, 'you will naturally wish to be the first to behold the restoration of Claire Baxter and hear whatever story she has to tell of her experiences whilst in a — er — deep freeze?'

'Naturally! Do I understand from that

that your husband has discovered a method of restoration?'

'No; I have. Purely inferred reasoning and I'm convinced it is right. I checked up with him at the Chief Inspector's office this morning and he believes I'm right. But, Sir James, I am one woman alone, fighting the toughest of battles. I have not a soul to help me, and obviously my husband cannot be released. The upshot is this: if I do not restore Claire — as I know I can with assistance — my husband, Dr. Campbell, and Nurse Addison will all be convicted, and probably medical science will lose the greatest discovery of all time.'

Sir James cleared his throat. He was neither old enough nor pompous enough not to be still swayed by the plaintive voice of a pretty blonde in distress.

'I sympathize with you deeply, madam,' he said gravely.

'Sympathy doesn't go far enough!' Eva insisted. 'It would take far too long to tell you everything over the 'phone, but I can explain this much: Claire, as you know, is in the furnace basement, whereas the switchboards and paraphernalia are in the surgery. It is absolutely essential that somebody with scientific knowledge — such as I'm sure you possess — help me to transfer the electrical equipment to the basement. And also lend a hand to link things up.'

'But why, dear lady? Would it not be simpler to put Miss Baxter back in the surgery? Haven't you, to use a vulgarism, rather got the cart before the horse?'

'Not by any means. There's a reason. Will you please help?'

'Well now — ' There seemed to be a lot of grumbling and puffing going on at the other end of the line. 'Consider my position as head of the Council — '

'That is exactly what I am doing, otherwise I wouldn't have called upon you to help. I want you to be first to see the restoration. After that you can handle things as you wish, using all your power as President to advertise the genius of my husband. In medical history you will be cited as the first man to behold a living being arising from a deep freeze.'

Masterly strategy! Eva felt quite warm

when she realized how much she had said, for her gift of oratory was almost non-existent. Desperation — plus a feeling that behind the highbrow Sir James was not such a bad old boy really — had given her unexpected if evanescent powers.

'I'll come!' Sir James declared promptly. 'I cannot afford to go through the rest of my life thinking that perhaps I was deaf when opportunity knocked. Expect me in — about half an hour.'

7

The Frozen Limit

Sir James was as good as his word, and well within half an hour his luxurious limousine pulled up outside the Cranston home. Without delay Eva opened the door to him and he looked a trifle surprised at the workmanlike outfit into which she had changed — slacks and a shirt blouse.

'I knew you wouldn't fail me, Sir James.' Eva pumped his hand up and down vigorously. 'If you'll come into the lounge I'll explain the situation. As a scientist and a doctor I'm sure you'll understand it.'

'I trust so indeed — '

Flattening his untidy gray hair, Sir James followed Eva into the lounge, but declined the drink she offered. Not that he was a teetotaler, but because he felt he would probably need all his wits about him for whatever was to follow.

'Well, it's like this — ' Eva sat on the settee opposite him and went into the details — so thoroughly indeed that the President's eyebrows rose once or twice in obvious admiration.

'And those are the facts,' Eva concluded. 'But for that power-line causing a dampening effect this trouble wouldn't have come about. You do see the urgency of the situation, I hope?'

'Certainly I do.' Sir James rose to his feet decisively. 'I'm more than willing to help, madam — and the sooner the better.'

Eva nodded in satisfaction and led the way to the door. Over her shoulder she said: 'The first thing to be done is to get the electrical equipment moved into the basement and linked up. It should be possible to do everything correctly if we follow out the wiring diagram in my husband's dossier.'

The President made an affirmative noise. It was so much safer than admitting that his knowledge of electrical matters was practically nil. Eva seemed to have made up her mind that he was a scientist, but he knew better than anybody that he was purely a medical man with none of the unusual gifts possessed by Bob Cranston.

Once in the surgery Eva looked about her, pointing to the various switchboards, and then the generator.

'These three have to go below — and that's all,' she said. 'The generator won't be easy, but it must be done. Ella will give us an extra hand.'

Sir James smiled rather uneasily and pulled off his jacket. Many years had passed since he had indulged in physical exercise in any great measure. It looked now as though he were going to catch up on those years in one grand slam. Eva, not in the least concerned with his reactions — seeing ahead of her only the accomplishment of her purpose — handed him one of two large wrenches.

'Here you are, Sir James. You unbolt one side of the generator and I'll tackle the other.'

'Yes indeed. Thank you.'

Having got his immaculate trousers

201

into position Sir James squatted and went to work.

'I suppose,' he asked as he strained and tugged on the huge nut locked in the wrench, 'that there is power laid on in the basement for a generator like this? Obviously you can't use a light socket, and that's the only power I've seen down there.'

Eva paused in her own efforts and looked troubled for a moment; then her face cleared. 'We shouldn't have any trouble in that direction. The power cable that comes up to this generator passes diagonally through the basement and is fastened to its wall. All we'll have to do will be to cut off the mains for a while, cut the main wire, and fasten it to this generator. I know enough about joining up electric wires to do that.'

'Splendid,' Sir James observed mechanically, and paused to mop his streaming face.

In thirty minutes the four nuts had been removed and the generator was ready to move. It seemed rather like trying to shift the world itself when Eva and the President tugged at it. It failed to budge in the slightest degree.

'This,' Sir James observed, his face wet and red, 'is not going to be easy, madam. I'll go further and say that it is impossible.'

Eva breathed hard. 'It hasn't got to be impossible, Sir James! Now you know why I wanted a man of the world to help me. I can't see the answer to this problem, but I'm sure you will.'

With the responsibility thus thrust upon him Sir James glowered in thought. Then, as a thought struck him, he smiled broadly.

'I believe, madam, there is a grating to the basement down which fuel is shot?'

Eva nodded. 'Pretty big one. It lies just left of the front door.'

The President strode to the surgery window and peered through it on to the wintry mid-day. Then he turned.

'The matter is not too difficult then. I have any number of labourers at my command since we are building an extension to the M.C. Headquarters. I'll have half a dozen of them here immediately after lunch, with equipment. Same sort of tackle as they use for moving a safe,' Sir James added vaguely. 'Seems to me it's only a matter of knocking this wall out, moving the generator along to the basement grating, and that's that.'

Eva did not dare say anything but she hoped devoutly that the laborers would remember to put the wall back in place afterwards. In any case nothing else signified at the moment except the restoration of Claire and the release of Bob. Eva was prepared to sacrifice the whole house to this end if necessary.

'As to these switchboards,' Sir James continued, 'I think we can manage them ourselves. At least we can try.'

Eva got the sneaking impression that he was actually commencing to enjoy himself. Perhaps he found this kind of manual work something of a relief from officialdom. Whatever it was he worked like a Trojan, and in half an hour he and Eva between them had unfastened the two principal switchboards from the wall and carefully wound up the cables, which would afterwards have to be connected to the tube.

So down into the basement, both of them working with the vigour of furniture removers. Ella saw them making the journey from the surgery, the second switchboard between them, and wondered whether or not she might not have been safer had she stayed at home to enjoy her enforced holiday. The Cranstons seemed to become crazier the longer she was with them.

'It is here,' Sir James observed, 'that we face our most exacting task, madam. Making sure the right connections are made. I don't feel quite up to the concentration before lunch, so I wonder if I — '

'You'll surely stay here for lunch?' Eva asked quickly. 'I have given Ella those instructions.'

'I had wondered, madam, if you would not prefer to dine with me?'

Eva hesitated, running her palms down her slacks. 'Well, normally I wouldn't think twice, but I'm thinking of the time we'll lose. I'd have to doll up and then get back into these glad rags — '

'Ah yes, indeed! I had overlooked that, Say no more, madam. I shall be only too happy to stay here to lunch. Now if you'll pardon me I'll 'phone for those labourers.'

Eva nodded and Sir James ascended the basement steps quickly. By the time he had finished 'phoning Eva had freshened herself up enough to be presentable. Ella brought in the lunch, but no time was wasted over consuming it. There was much to be done, and as far as Sir James himself was concerned he felt that he dared not take too long away from his official duties. So, less than half an hour after lunch had been served, the two were back in the basement, carefully checking the cables and the various terminals on the tube to which they applied.

So far all was well. One by one the connections were made; then towards two o'clock the laborers arrived. They came in a truck upon which were also a winch, block and tackle, and lengths of steel cable and trolleys such as are used for moving pianos. Eva noted all this, left the arranging to Sir James, and went back into the basement to continue the linking up.

Thereafter, for over an hour, concussions shook the house. The wall of the surgery was smashed down, its upper half being supported on makeshift beams; then the heavy generator was man-handled out into the front garden — to the interest of neighbors and passers-by — and so finally lowered through the basement grating, which had to be enlarged to permit of passage.

Mentally closing her ears against the din and occasional swearing from the workmen, Eva kept on with the job of making connections. She only paused once, and this was when she threw a dustsheet over the tube so no comments could be made about the delectable, lightly-clad girl within it.

Three o'clock and the generator was in position. Four o'clock and the concrete was hardening around the bolts which would hold it in place. Five o'clock and the workmen had gone, the wall of the surgery rebuilt and the basement grating restored to its normal dimensions.

'Quite an upset!' Sir James observed, his dirty face endeavoring to look genial. 'I am sure your husband will be astonished when he hears of the trouble you have been to.'

Eva gave him a serious glance. 'I'm not thinking of any of the side issues, Sir James. I'm only too grateful that I had the good sense to contact a man as reliable as you. None of this could have been accomplished without you.'

Sir James beamed, quite unconscious of the fact that this soft-soaping had been thrown in, in an effort to make sure he would see the thing through to the finish.

'We'd better give these cables a final check-over,' Eva said, tightening the last terminal in the circuit. 'I think everything else is more or less in order.'

Together they went to work once more, following everything from Bob's original diagram. Fortunately the greatest intricacy was concerned with the actual wiring of the switchboards themselves. The main cables leading from it were not difficult to select, particularly as they were all picked out in different colours.

'That's it,' Sir James confirmed finally. 'Every wire in its right place — ' He prodded the edge of the concrete around the generator. 'In about another hour this should be hard enough to stand the generator being started up. Then we can make the effort at restoration.'

Eva sighed and relaxed a little. 'That's all I'm waiting for! We'd better rest awhile and have a meal — if you can still spare time?'

'I may as well be hung for a sheep as a lamb now, madam. Believe me, I am looking forward to this evening with as much eagerness as a schoolboy!'

* * *

Actually, it was nearly three hours later, not far from nine o'clock, before the concrete had set sufficiently for the generator to be started up. To have attempted it without a solid base might have had unpredictable consequences. But now everything was ready. The interval of time had been well spent by both Eva and Sir James. They had made it the occasion to thoroughly study the method of procedure outlined by Bob.

The critical moment had arrived. Eva herself took charge of the switchboards that would control the restoration. Sir James took over the task of watching the reaction meters.

'I am ready, Mrs. Cranston, when you are,' he said finally.

Eva gave a brief nod, the tautness of her face showing how much strain she was undergoing. One mistake now, a misinterpretation of what her husband had written down and Claire Baxter's life might be sacrificed. Then Eva set her firm little jaw and closed the main switch. It was a stunning shock when nothing happened. The generator should have begun to whine and creep up the scale to full rhythm. Instead — nothing.

'Something's wrong!' Eva seemed to positively wilt as she looked across at Sir James.

'Obviously,' he agreed, not in the least shaken. 'We must discover what it is and put it right. Mmm, let me see now — '

It only took him about five seconds to find the fault. He even smiled broadly.

'It is always a good idea to have power connected to get a result,' he commented. 'Observe!'

Eva followed the line of his pointing finger and then gave a shaken laugh. In the general rush of making sure the generator was firmly bedded, and connecting its various cables to the switchboards, the power wire which must feed it — and which went up to the surgery where it had now been insulated off — had not been attached. It lay there undisturbed, secured to the wall.

'We forgot it,' Sir James observed, pulling out his penknife. 'If you'll cut the power and find some insulating tape we can soon put things right.'

Eva wasted no time. First she had Ella bring a couple of lighted candles; then the power was cut at the mains. The rest was up to Sir James. Laboriously, with pliers and penknife, he severed the cable and bared the ends, after which the needed connection to the generator was completed and bound up with several yards of insulating tape. The join was a makeshift one at the best: it might even burn out under the load, but that was one of the things that had to be risked.

'Right!' Sir James announced finally. 'On with the power and let's try again!'

Ella, who was waiting above for this signal, immediately hurried to the hall fuse box and snapped on the main switch. The lights in the basement returned.

'Here we go again,' Eva murmured, and closed the make-and-break switch. Immediately the generator hummed and then swiftly rose to the steady whine of maximum. Sir James gave a delighted glance but made no comment.

Within the tube nothing, so far, had happened. Eva looked at the open dossier beside her, making sure once again what to do next. Finally she turned back to the number two switchboard and moved the controls in the order stated. The filigree of wires around the tube immediately started to glow. The contact points shone brightly. Electric energy surged and then died away again

'Any reaction?' Eva demanded tensely, and Sir James kept a steady eye on the meters.

'Not yet. Heartbeats sixteen per minute. Temperature minus one twenty Fahrenheit. That represents no change in conditions.'

Eva looked again at the dossier and so entered stage two of the restoration process. She quickly snapped down four buttons on the top of the panel, in response to which the energy reaching the tube obviously increased.

'Seventeen!' Sir James cried in exultaion. Then: 'Eighteen! Heartbeats are becoming faster — By heaven, this is wonderful! Temperature has risen one-eighteen. We're on the right track!'

Keeping her emotions well in hand Eva still went systematically about her task, following the dossier directions for every move she made. There was no doubt now, though, that the reversal process was operating correctly. With the passage of the seconds the temperature rose steadily and the increase in Claire's heartbeats and respiration kept exact step — until at length Eva had made all the possible moves on the switchboards and there was nothing left for her to do but watch the outcome. She moved across to the tube and stood gazing tensely within it.

She found it a fascinating, sobering experience. As she stood watching, the frost within the tube gradually faded away into moisture, and that too at length dried away into vapor and passed off through vents specially contrived for the purpose. Sir James, eager though he was to take a look at the girl, remained rigidly at his post before the meters.

'Sixty-eight beats to the minute!' he exclaimed finally. 'Temperature nearing seventy degrees, which is almost the heat of this basement. We've done it, Mrs. Cranston. No doubt of that!'

When at last the register showed the normal seventy-two heartbeats to the minute he deserted his post and moved to Eva's side to watch the miracle with her. And miracle it certainly was, for this girl had been restored without harm from a state of absolute frozen solidity. Now that glaze had left her flesh and it had become of the normal creamy whiteness appropriate to her age and type. Into her face crept a faint flush of colour, so gradual it was almost undetectable in its increase — and it was at this point that the hum of the generator suddenly ceased.

Instantly Sir James wheeled in alarm, staring at it. Then Eva's taut, excited voice reassured him.

'Nothing to worry about, Sir James. According to the dossier the machinery automatically cuts itself out on the thermostatic principle once the correct level has been reached.'

'Thank heaven for that! I thought the apparatus had broken down at the vital moment — Yes, yes, I remember reading about the automatic cut-out.' Sir James mopped his face quickly.

Then Claire opened her eyes — not slowly like one aroused from sleep, but as though she had suddenly been called by name.

'That's all we need!' Eva cried in delight, nearly dancing a hornpipe. 'The instruments showed she was alive, but this is visible proof! We'd better get the tube open!'

Sir James was already doing so, spinning the wing-nuts swiftly and then taking off the heavy cover. The airtight rubber sheath followed and the end of the tube was wide open with Claire's mass of golden hair facing towards him.

'Are — are you all right, young woman?' he asked, hesitantly.

Within the tube Claire smiled. 'Of course I'm all right. Is there any reason why I shouldn't be?'

'Every reason, if you but knew it,' Eva murmured. 'Out you get — if you can.'

Which was not so easy. In the first instance Claire had had to be 'inserted' in the tube: now the opposite performance was called for. She pushed with her bare feet until her head emerged, then Sir James fussed uncertainly at the vision of bare arms and shoulders sliding towards him.

'Er — perhaps you — ' He looked hopefully at Eva. She gave a nod, seized Claire firmly under the arms and tugged. In a moment she had slithered headlong out of the tube and then stood up.

'Thanks,' she said gaily, saluting Eva. 'Easier to get into than out of. I was — ' She broke off, gazing in wonderment about her, then moving her bare feet up and down uncomfortably on the concrete floor. 'What the dickens has happened? I'll swear the surgery didn't look like this!'

'This is the basement,' Eva told her, and Sir James cleared his throat as he surveyed the brevity of Claire's swimsuit.

'You'll be cold like that, my dear.'

'Cold? Not a bit. Quite warm in here — '

'Gown coming up,' Eva said, reaching to one of her own set aside for the purpose. 'And a pair of slippers.'

'Thanks. Very kind of you.' Claire got into them and pushed the hair out of her eyes. Her pretty face was still puzzled. 'Look, there's an awful lot here which I don't understand. I don't know either you or this gentleman. And I certainly did not go to sleep in the coal cellar!'

Eva smiled rather tiredly. 'I'm Mrs. Cranston, Claire — '

'Oh, good! I wondered what you'd be

like.' Claire shook hands and waited for the next — which was a handshake with Sir James, dirty but beaming.

'My husband, Dr. Campbell and Nurse Addison are all under arrest for presumably having murdered you,' Eva added, and as Claire's wide blue eyes went even wider, Eva explained in detail. Instead of the sober reaction she expected, Claire burst into hysterical laughter.

'Frankly,' Eva said solemnly, 'I cannot see anything at all funny in the situation.'

'Probably not, because you've had all the worry and hard work. What is tickling me is the thought of those two boys — and they're such decent fellows, both of them — being had for killing me and all I did was dream beautifully and take it easy! Money for jam!'

'Dream?' Sir James asked quickly. 'Ah, that is what we want to get at, Miss Baxter. Your exact reactions whilst under the deep freeze — '

'I think we'll discuss in the lounge,' Eva put in. 'This is hardly the place, and I should imagine you're both tired and hungry, Claire?'

'Hungry, yes. Tired? Not a bit.'

She moved actively to the basement stairs and Eva and Sir James followed her up. The faithful Ella was called in to provide immediate refreshment, and it said much for her self-control that she did not even blink when she beheld the formerly frozen girl at her ease in the armchair.

'The whole world is going to acclaim you, Miss Baxter,' Sir James enthused. 'By your extreme courage you have proved that deep-freeze anaesthesia — and I think we may call it that — is a definitely practicable thing. For myself I always felt it was, but as the President of the M.C. I am not entitled to a personal opinion. At least I wasn't then. Now it is very, very different!'

'This means then,' Claire asked, 'that suspended animation can be used on people in need of major operations and things?'

'Definitely! A new era in surgery, made possible by your bravery — '

'Never mind my bravery,' Claire smiled. 'Think of the brains of Dr. Cranston to think of such a thing! I don't think Borry Campbell could have thought up such a discovery. He's more romantic than brainy.'

'I'll go and 'phone the Yard,' Eva said quickly, rising. 'I must let the Inspector know immediately that everything's all right. I'll also ask them to get in touch with your brother — he must be worried sick.'

Claire smiled faintly. 'I doubt it! Jimmy's not the type.'

Eva hurried from the room and Sir James coughed primly.

'Whilst in this freeze, Miss Baxter, wherein you were reduced to a temperature of minus one-twenty below zero, did you not feel anything? Was the slow-down of your molecular structure complete?'

She shrugged. 'I suppose so. I don't know anything about molecular structure, though Dr. Cranston and Borry Campbell said a lot about it before they experimented. My reaction was just that of sliding down peacefully into sleep. I didn't even feel cold. Just drowsy, and happy, and then — then I dreamed.

Quiet, interesting dreams. Nothing startling. They didn't seem to last above a few seconds before I found myself awake again.'

'Amazing — yet how wonderful!' Sir James sat brooding as Ella brought in sandwiches and coffee. 'This means that all the old anaesthetic systems are finished with. A patient need fear nothing. Just gentle sleep, bloodless surgery, and the surgeon himself having all the time he needs to complete his job without fear of the patient dying before restoration can take place. The world has reason to be eternally grateful to you, young woman — and to Dr. Cranston, of course.'

Eva returned quickly into the lounge, her face bright.

'I've told the Inspector everything, Sir James. He was waiting in his office in case some news came through. He says it means Bob, Dr. Campbell and Nurse Addison will be released immediately. First he's coming to check things for himself and bringing the Assistant Commissioner with him. By tomorrow, or sooner, Bob will be back home.'

Sir James smiled. 'You have reason to feel proud, madam, of your own endeavours. When I give my full statement to the Medical Council, I shall see to it that you receive your full measure of praise.'

'Do you know,' Claire asked, glancing up, 'if Dr. Campbell will come back here with your husband, Mrs. Cranston, or will he go to his own home?'

Eva shrugged. 'No idea. I should think he'll most certainly come here first to see the miracle for himself. You must stay the night, Claire, and we'll fix things up properly tomorrow.'

'Yes.' Claire smiled to herself. 'Thanks, I will.'

'A doctor's wife is always prepared for any eventuality,' Eva added, seating herself. 'Otherwise I don't think I could so easily have accepted you in my home. At first it was a bit of a shock.'

'I'm sure,' Claire sympathized, tackling the sandwiches. 'At least being a doctor's wife helps to stop things getting too monotonous, I imagine.'

In six months Claire Campbell had no need to imagine the life of a doctor's wife.

She was having first hand experience, and enjoying it. The only thing that Boris Campbell refused to accept from her was her declaration that she was 'The Frozen Limit.'

'Not now, perhaps,' she admitted. 'But I was once — and look at the result! The whole medical world using the Cranston Deep Freeze System! It was worth being the Frozen Limit to have given so much hope to a suffering world.'

THE END

Books by John Russell Fearn
in the Linford Mystery Library:

THE TATTOO MURDERS
VISION SINISTER
THE SILVERED CAGE
WITHIN THAT ROOM!
REFLECTED GLORY
THE CRIMSON RAMBLER
SHATTERING GLASS
THE MAN WHO WAS NOT
ROBBERY WITHOUT VIOLENCE
DEADLINE
ACCOUNT SETTLED
STRANGER IN OUR MIDST
WHAT HAPPENED TO HAMMOND?
THE GLOWING MAN
FRAMED IN GUILT
FLASHPOINT
THE MASTER MUST DIE
DEATH IN SILHOUETTE
THE LONELY ASTRONOMER
THY ARM ALONE
MAN IN DUPLICATE
THE RATTENBURY MYSTERY

We do hope that you have enjoyed reading this large print book.

Did you know that all of our titles are available for purchase?

We publish a wide range of high quality large print books including:
Romances, Mysteries, Classics
General Fiction
Non Fiction and Westerns

Special interest titles available in large print are:
The Little Oxford Dictionary
Music Book, Song Book
Hymn Book, Service Book

Also available from us courtesy of Oxford University Press:
Young Readers' Dictionary
(large print edition)
Young Readers' Thesaurus
(large print edition)

For further information or a free brochure, please contact us at:
Ulverscroft Large Print Books Ltd.,
The Green, Bradgate Road, Anstey,
Leicester, LE7 7FU, England.
Tel: (00 44) **0116 236 4325**
Fax: (00 44) **0116 234 0205**